PURRFECT HEAT

THE MYSTERIES OF MAX 4

NIC SAINT

PUSS IN PRINT PUBLICATIONS

PURRFECT HEAT

The Mysteries of Max 4

Copyright © 2017 by Nic Saint

Edited by Chereese Graves

www.nicsaint.com

Give feedback on the book at: info@nicsaint.com

facebook.com/nicsaintauthor
@nicsaintauthor

First Edition

Printed in the U.S.A

PROLOGUE

*E*rin Coka arrived bright and early for work. It was her day to open *Fry Me for an Oyster* and she didn't want to be late. As a newish employee of the restaurant, she had everything to prove and everything to lose. Not that her employers, Brainard and Isabella Stowe, were terrible people or anything. They just ran a tight ship, and expected all members of their staff, from the dishwashers to the chef, to do the work and show up on time.

Lately, things had been even more hectic than usual, with the famous celebrity chef Niklaus Skad in town, subjecting *Fry Me for an Oyster* to his usual grueling treatment. He'd been all over the place, a camera crew in tow, criticizing the menus, the seating, the decorations, the presentation and even the way the staff dressed and behaved. It seemed nothing was good enough for the Great Niklaus, and Brainard and Isabella had been on edge all week. *Kitchen Disasters* could make or break their business, though by the looks of things, Niklaus was leaning more toward destroying them.

Erin opened the door and stepped inside. The air was

stale and musty—redolent with cooking scents. She stuck her nose in the air and sniffed. Yuck. Something smelled awful. Had Hendrik been working on one of his notorious creations again? Cooking up something special for Niklaus? Going for a last-ditch attempt to save his career and the restaurant?

She walked through to the kitchen. "Chef? Chef, are you in here?"

Sometimes, when the mood struck him, Hendrik Serarols liked to come in at the crack of dawn to try out a few new recipes he'd dreamed up. She walked past the bar and through the swinging doors into the large kitchen at the back. Here Hendrik created his masterpieces, which had put *Fry Me for an Oyster* on the map in Hampton Cove and far beyond.

"Yuck," she muttered, as her eyes scanned the squeaky clean kitchen.

All gleaming countertops and scrubbed pots dangling over the stoves. Everything perfectly clean, as it should be. Niklaus Skad was big on hygiene, his pet peeve. The stench seemed to be coming from one of the ovens, the biggest one, where they baked pizza and other large dishes. Hendrik had once joked you could fit a man in there, even one as big as him.

She walked over to the oven and saw that it was switched on. "Chef?" she repeated. "Are you cooking something in here?" No reply.

She peered in through the oven window. Whatever it was, it had been cooking for so long that smoke was curling out through the vents. Had Chef put something in last night and forgotten to turn off the oven? He had so much on his mind lately he was starting to get a little frazzled. And who could blame him? With Niklaus on his case all the time, even yelling and screaming, and the camera crew in his face while

2

he tried to keep it together and run the kitchen, a lesser man would have fallen to pieces.

She flicked on the oven light, and that's when she saw it. Her lips parted on a silent scream. There was a man in there, baked to a crisp!

CHAPTER 1

J was luxuriating in my all-time favorite spot: at the foot of Odelia's bed. I'm blessed with a smallish human, which means I've got the foot of the bed all to myself. I've heard horror stories of other cats, whose owners stretch out all the way to the edge of the bed, and then wriggle around all night, making it absolutely impossible for any cat to get any sleep.

In that sense, Odelia is the perfect human. Well, not just because she's short, but also because she's super nice and sweet. She always makes sure I'm well fed and well taken care of, never stingy on the cuddles and the strokes, and she keeps my blorange fur looking nice and shiny by giving me a vigorous grooming every week without fail. She's even installed a pet door so I can come and go as I please. A nice, big door, as I'm big-boned.

Odelia is a reporter for the Hampton Cove Gazette, and if there's one thing that sets her aside from most humans, it's that she speaks feline. Yep, she and I have a perfect under-standing—literally. She takes care of me, and in return I collect gossip from all over town and give it to her hot off the griddle. All the news that's fit to print, straight from the cat's mouth.

Odelia stirred, and I pricked up my ears. I can tell when she's about to wake up, which is my cue to snuggle up to her and bury my nose in her armpit for an extra cuddle. It's our morning ritual, and the start of our day.

This morning, however, things were going to prove different, and the first sign I got was when Dooley and Brutus came barging into the bedroom, looking excited, but not in a good way.

Dooley is my best bud, a gray Raggamuffin who belongs to Odelia's Gran. Brutus is a black cat and... not exactly my buddy. He belongs to Chase Kingsley, a cop and occasional kissmate of Odelia's. Yes, I know kissmate isn't a word, but how else can I describe Chase and Odelia's relationship? They're not a couple, they just... kiss... sometimes. And flirt a lot, I guess. I know, it's disgusting, but what can you do? Humans are weird that way.

"Max!" Dooley cried. "Terrible news! Terrible, terrible news!"

I reluctantly heaved my head from the soft blanket. "What is it?" I murmured, then yawned cavernously. Dooley is one of those overexcited cats who get their tail in a twist just because their human got them a new brand of kibble or a new smell of cat litter.

"A new cat," Dooley said, still panting. "There's a new cat in town."

I looked from Dooley to Brutus, who was, at least in my eyes, still the new cat in town, even though by now he'd been here a couple of months.

"No, not me," Brutus grunted. "A new new cat."

I frowned. "So? New cats are born every day. What's so special about this one?"

"He's not a kitten," Dooley announced, looking highly perturbed.

"He's a full-grown cat," said Brutus. "And he belongs to Chase."

"Your Chase?"

"My Chase."

"That's not possible. Your Chase doesn't even like cats. He just took you in because his mother is living with her sister who's allergic to cats."

It was a long story. Brutus had belonged to Chase's mom, but when she couldn't take care of him anymore, Chase had graciously agreed to give him a home. Though he spent most of his time either at Odelia's or next door, at Odelia's mom's place, where Dooley lives with Gran.

"Martha loves cats," Brutus explained. "She just can't help herself. So when she saw this rascal roaming the streets, she took him home with her, and immediately got into a huge argument with her sister."

"So Chase took him over? Again?" I asked, incredulous.

Brutus nodded somberly. "And he's something else, this one."

"He's called Diego and he's a real charmer. A regular ladies' cat."

"Like Brutus, you mean," I said, giving Brutus a level look.

"I'm not a ladies' cat," Brutus protested. "Can I help it that the ladies all love me? It's not as if I go out of my way to seduce them or anything. They just take one look at me and bingo. They go all gooey on me."

"That's a ladies' cat," I said in measured tones. "That's you."

"You got it all wrong as usual, Maxie, baby," Brutus growled.

"No, you got it all wrong. As usual," I countered.

"No, you got it all wrong!"

"No, you got it—"

"It doesn't matter!" Dooley cried. "Diego is here and Harriet is going to take one look at him and she's going to go weak at the knees and fall for him!"

"Not my Harriet," Brutus said, though he didn't look convinced.

"Your Harriet?" Dooley asked. "Harriet isn't your Harriet."

"Oh, yes, she is. I know you're devastated by the fact that she likes me more than you, but she is mine," said Brutus with a smirk. "All mine."

"Harriet isn't yours. Harriet is a free spirit. She belongs to no one."

"All mine," he said in a sing-songy voice. "All the time."

"Where is Harriet, by the way?" I asked.

Harriet belongs to Odelia's mom and also lives next door. She's a white Persian with green eyes. Even though she's totally not my type I have to admit she's very pretty. And she likes to hang out with Brutus, he wasn't lying about that. Much to Dooley's chagrin, cause he's got a crush on Harriet himself.

"I have no idea," said Brutus. "When I woke up just now she wasn't there."

I cut a glance at Dooley, and he nodded somberly. Brutus had taken to spending the night at the house, occupying the spot next to Harriet on the bed. When they weren't traipsing all over town, that was.

Odelia muttered something, and I wasn't surprised. All this meowing and hissing had probably woken her up. "Now see what you've done," I said. "You've gone and woken up my human."

"What do you care?" Brutus asked. "She needs to get up anyway."

"I like her to wake up gradually."

"Max likes to snuggle with Odelia," said Dooley. "He's a snuggler."

It's a good thing us cats are covered with fur, otherwise Brutus would have noticed the blush that was now creeping up my cheeks.

"I am not," I said indignantly. "You take that back, Dooley."

"I'm not taking it back. You are a snuggler. You like to snuggle."

"Nothing to be ashamed about, Maxie," said Brutus with a sly grin. "Some cats are snugglers and others aren't. I for one would never want to be caught dead trying to stick my nose in Chase's armpit, or sniff at his hair. Yuck. I mean, don't get me wrong, I like the guy, but that's not how we roll."

"So how do you roll?" I asked, giving him my best scowl.

He studied his claws. "You know, us catly cats just hang, you know. Like bros. Like buds. Chase, Chief Alec and I like to watch the ballgame, knocking back a few brewskis, swapping some off-color stories from our sordid pasts. It's what real cats do. You wouldn't understand."

"You don't drink brewskis," I said heatedly. "And you definitely don't swap off-color stories about your sordid past because Chase doesn't speak feline and neither does Uncle Alec. You're making all that up."

He grinned. "Keep telling yourself that. Whatever makes you feel good, bro. Just keep on snuggling. Nothing wrong with that. Nothing at all."

"There is nothing wrong with that!" I cried.

"That's what I just said."

"No, but you said it in a way that makes it sound wrong!"

"Hey, don't you go getting all weird on me, Maxie. I said I'm fine with you being all feminine and girly so why don't you just let me be all manly and butch, huh? To each his own is what I always say."

9

I narrowed my eyes at him, and I was itching to give him a piece of my mind—or my claws. Then again, Brutus is a formidable cat. Strong and athletic. I may be bigger, but I'm not afraid to admit it's mostly blubber.

"Easy there, big guy," said Brutus, catching my glare and holding up his paws in a peaceable gesture. "You look like you're about to blow a gasket. We're all buds here, okay?"

"Right," I said dubiously.

"Do you really drink beer, Brutus?" Dooley asked.

"Of course. You're not a real cat if you haven't downed some suds."

"I haven't downed some suds," said Dooley. "You think I should try?"

"First chance you get," Brutus assured him. "But go easy, slugger. Not everyone can stomach the stuff."

"Let me guess," I said. "Only real cats can, right?"

"That's right, Maxie. Though if you can't keep it down, that's fine, too."

He was playing with me, as usual, and I wondered if this new cat was going to be just like Brutus, for if he was, Dooley was right. This was bad.

Just then, the doorbell rang, and I groaned. Now I was never going to get my morning cuddle. Brutus grinned at me. He'd read my mind.

Odelia murmured something, smacked her lips, and sat upright in bed, blinking confusedly. When she saw us, she blinked some more. "Um, Max? Are there really three of you or am I seeing things?"

"You're not seeing things," I said. "Dooley and Brutus came over."

"Oh, hi, Dooley—Brutus."

The doorbell rang again.

"There it is," she said. "I thought I'd heard something."

With her blond hair a mess, her green eyes trying hard to

focus, and her nose wrinkling in confusion, my human looked cute as a button. She swung her feet to the *Finding Nemo* carpet by the bed, and I saw she was wearing her pink Betty Boop pajamas. She staggered from the bed, and shuffled to the door.

"So what were you guys talking about?" she asked as she stumbled down the stairs, rubbing at her eyes with one hand while holding onto the banister with the other.

"About the new cat," Dooley said.

"His name is Diego and he's a real charmer," I said. "At least according to Brutus."

"Well, he is," Brutus said. "I only talked to him for all of five minutes and I could see he was one of those ladies' cats."

"You mean like you," Odelia said, not missing a beat.

"I'm not a ladies' cat!" Brutus cried. "Ladies just like me!"

"That's a ladies' cat," I said.

"Diego belongs to Chase," Dooley said.

Odelia halted on the bottom step and looked down at Dooley. "Chase has a new cat?"

"Used to belong to his mother, just like Brutus," I explained. I gave her a worried look. She nodded. She understood Dooley and I didn't like Brutus. And if this new cat was anything like him, we were in for another nasty surprise.

"I'm sure Diego will prove to be a perfectly nice cat," she said.

Odelia is always the picture of optimism. For her the glass is always half-full. You have to admire that about her, of course. Then again, sometimes the glass is half-empty. Or completely empty. Like in the case of Brutus.

Odelia made her way to the door and peeked through the peephole.

"Oh," she said, surprised, and quickly turned and looked in the hallway mirror. "Ugh," she said, and finger-combed her hair and checked her eyes for sleep gunk. Then she heaved a resigned sigh and opened the door. Odelia's uncle Alec stood on the mat, along with Chase Kingsley, who was holding up a small orange cat.

"That's Diego!" hissed Brutus.

"Surprise," said Chase with a smile, and handed the cat to Odelia.

CHAPTER 2

*O*delia took the cat from Chase. She was feeling a little awkward. If only she'd known they were coming over, she could have splashed some water on her face, sprayed some deodorant on her pits and dressed in something a little more appropriate than her Betty Boop pajamas.

"Sleeping in?" asked her uncle Alec with a grin as he stepped inside.

"I must have slept through my alarm," she said. "What time is it?"

"Seven thirty," said Chase, following her uncle in.

"Oh." Her alarm had been set for eight, so it wasn't that she was late. They were early. "So what brings you here?" She held up the cat. "Showing off this little guy?"

"He's my mom's," Chase said apologetically. He wasn't dressed in his pajamas but in jeans, a plaid shirt and boots. With his slightly tousled dark hair, clear blue eyes and chiseled features he was like an all-out assault of manliness. A lot to take in before breakfast.

"So... you want me to take care of him for a while?" she guessed.

He grimaced. "Thing is, since Brutus spends more time over here than at your uncle's place, I just figured you might have room for another one?"

"Sure," she said, setting down the cat. Max and Dooley looked dumbfounded, and Brutus downright hostile, but she didn't care. They'd just have to learn to get along. Just like she and Chase had done. When the cop had first arrived in town, he hadn't liked that Odelia occasionally got involved in her uncle's police investigations. As a former NYPD detective, that kind of thing simply wasn't done. Now, however, they got on just fine.

"We're not here about the cat, honey," Chief Alec said with a grimace.

Uh-oh. She knew that look. "Something happened, right? Something bad?"

"Afraid so," said Chase. "Have you ever watched Niklaus Skad's *Kitchen Disasters*?"

"Where he humiliates and destroys restaurant owners for entertainment purposes? I've seen it once or twice. Not my cup of tea."

"Well, looks like someone didn't like him."

"Niklaus Skad was murdered? In Hampton Cove?"

"He was here to tape a segment of his show at *Fry Me for an Oyster*," said Chase. "He was found this morning, stuck in the restaurant oven."

"Completely cooked," Uncle Alec added, shaking his head.

"Yikes. That's a horrible way to go." But also very apt, of course.

"We're going out there right now," said Chase. "So we figured you might want to tag along."

She stared at him. Was he serious? Not all that long ago the mere thought that a reporter would tag along with him would have gotten him madder than a wet hen. And now he was actually inviting her to join him? He'd definitely had a change of heart. Then again, she'd helped him crack a few cases since they first met. And had even done him a personal favor by getting him absolved of a phony molestation charge hanging over his head.

Uncle Alec was grinning at her from behind Chase's back, and gave her a wink. "Sure," she said finally. "I'd love to come. Um… I need to change into something more appropriate first, though."

Chase smiled. "Why? I love me some Betty Boop."

"Me, too," she said. "But it doesn't really inspire confidence. People might think I'm a flake."

"A cute flake," Chase said, rocking back on his heels.

She gave him a curious glance. He was awfully cheerful this morning. Probably happy something was finally happening in Hampton Cove. For the former NYPD detective life in the small town was probably boring.

"If you're gonna change you better do it now," her uncle said, tapping his watch.

"Be back in a jiffy," she said, and bounded up the stairs.

For the next fifteen minutes she showered, dressed and even took the time to apply some makeup. She might be about to meet lying suspects, heinous criminals and a very dead murder victim, but that didn't mean she had to look like crap. And then there was Chase, of course. He might like her in her Betty Boop outfit, but she just knew she could do a whole lot better. Not that she wanted to impress him. Not her. Nah-uh.

"So why let me tag along?" she asked, scooting up the backseat of her uncle's squad car while he put the car in gear and pulled away.

Chase turned to face her, putting his elbow on the headrest. "It's like I told your uncle. You've got a knack for it,

15

Odelia. I've never known anyone who's got a knack for solving murders like you have. You're a natural."

"Apart from Jessica Fletcher," her uncle said, keeping his eye on the road.

"Yes, well, your niece is a lot easier on the eyes than Jessica."

Was he flirting with her? Not that she was complaining. "Thanks for the compliment," she said. "Though I'm sure you're just exaggerating."

"About what?" asked her uncle with a twinkle in his eye. "The sleuthing thing or the easier on the eyes thing?"

"Both," she said. "I mean, I just get lucky from time to time, I guess."

"We both know luck's got nothing to do with it," said Chase. "You have a knack, Odelia, and I would be an idiot not to make good use of it."

He gave her a penetrating look that sent her heart rate rocketing up.

"I'm glad you're finally seeing things my way, Chase," said Chief Alec. "It sure took you long enough."

"Yes, well, where I come from civilians don't butt into police investigations," he said stubbornly, repeating his old line. "They just don't," he repeated when the chief shook his head and uttered a groan.

"Where you come from they don't have girls like my niece," Alec said.

"That's true enough," Chase agreed with another sly look at her.

"So what about this murder?" she asked, deciding to get this conversation out of the gutter. "What have you found out so far?"

Chase took a notebook from his shirt pocket. "Murder was reported by Erin Coka. She's a waitress and was opening

16

up the restaurant this morning. Said she thought the chef had forgotten to turn off the oven."

"Who's the chef?"

"Hendrik Serarols. So far hasn't shown up for work."

"Which is suspicious," her uncle said with a nod.

"Who owns *Fry Me for an Oyster*?" She'd never been there, but had heard good things about it.

Chase read from his notebook again. "Brainard and Isabella Stowe. It's their third restaurant. The previous two went belly-up. This one was a success."

"A big success," Uncle Alec confirmed. "Which is why it got the attention of Niklaus Skad. The man likes to attach his name to success stories."

"And then tear them down," Odelia said, remembering some snippets from *Kitchen Disasters*. The man was unrelenting and brutal. She wondered what had induced the Stowes to feature on his show. Then again, any publicity was good publicity, probably. She wasn't a marketing expert, but being on TV was probably the best way of getting your name out there.

They'd arrived at the restaurant, which was on Norfolk Street, and her uncle parked across the street. Uniformed officers were blocking anyone from entering the restaurant, and were keeping onlookers at bay.

"Did you let your cats out, Odelia?" asked her uncle, locking eyes with her through the rearview mirror.

"I've got a pet door," she said. "They come and go as they please."

"Good," he said with a nod.

"I didn't know you were so concerned about cats, Chief?" asked Chase, surprised.

The Chief shrugged. "What can I say? I'm a softie at heart."

But Odelia knew why he'd asked. Unlike Chase, her uncle knew the secret of her sleuthing success. She had two assistants working for her, scouring the streets for clues: Max and Dooley. Cats are everywhere, and since people rarely hold back in front of them, they harbor a lot of secrets, and don't mind sharing those secrets with other cats... like Max and Dooley.

They crossed the street. Chase and her uncle went in to check the crime scene and talk to the coroner. She stayed behind. She'd spotted what she assumed were the owners of the restaurant, and decided to have a chat.

Brainard Stowe was a stout man with a comb-over, who stood nervously hopping from one leg to the other while an officer took the couple's statement. His wife Isabella was the motherly type, and reminded Odelia of her own mother. She was round with a kind face and overly large glasses, and was dressed in a floral print dress that seemed ill-fitted to keep her ample curves in check. She and her husband looked like they'd been rudely awakened, had put on the first thing they found, and had rushed over.

She waited patiently until the couple had given their statement, and approached them with a friendly smile. "Hi. My name is Odelia Poole. I'm a reporter for the Hampton Cove Gazette and a civilian consultant with the Hampton Cove Police Department. Can you tell me what happened?"

The woman's eyes were red-rimmed, and it was obvious she'd been crying. Her husband, on the other hand, appeared incensed for some reason.

"I know who you are," Isabella said. "I love your articles, Miss Poole."

"I can't believe this," Brainard said. "When are they going to let us in?"

"Not until the crime scene has been thoroughly examined and the coroner has taken away the body," I said.

His eyes shifted to me. "You're Chief Alec's niece, aren't you? Can't you ask him when I can reopen my restaurant?"

"You can ask him yourself, honey," said his wife. "I'm sure he'll want to talk to us once he's through in there."

"I hope they're not going to close us down for a week," he grumbled. "Something like this can wreck a business. And I know a thing or two about wrecking a business."

Isabella smiled nervously. "I'm sure Miss Poole doesn't want to know about all of that, honey," she said, placing a warning hand on his arm.

"Mh? Oh. Right," he said, realizing he wasn't talking to himself.

"Is it true that Niklaus Skad was filming his show *Kitchen Disasters* in your restaurant?" I asked.

"Yes," said Isabella. "We made the arrangements last fall, and filming had just started a couple of days ago."

"And how would you describe the experience?"

Brainard frowned. "Rotten. I wish we'd never agreed to do his damn show." Isabella put her hand on his arm again but he shook it off. "And I don't care who knows it. You can print this on your front page for all I care. Niklaus Skad was a horrible human being who got off on hurting others. A failed and bitter restaurateur who took out his rancor on other, more successful business owners. He bullied our chef, he bullied our staff, he bullied us, heck, he even bullied our cat! The man was a well-dressed thug!"

"I hope you're not going to write that in your article, Miss Poole," Isabella said. "Brainard is overwrought. He doesn't mean what he says."

"I mean every word! I think whoever killed the man deserves a medal!"

"Keep your voice down," Isabella hissed. "The police are here."

"They know we didn't do it," said Brainard. "How could

we? We were..." His pale blue eyes shifted to me again, and he promptly clamped his mouth shut.

"Yes?" I prompted. "You were..."

"We were home last night," said Isabella. "All night."

"Can anyone vouch for you?" I asked. "I mean, I'm sure my uncle will want to know."

Husband and wife shared a quick glance, then Isabella produced a nervous giggle. "I—we—well, the thing is..."

"You don't have to tell her," Brainard said. "There's such a thing as privacy in this country. There are laws and stuff."

"Privacy is the first thing that goes out the window when a dead body is found stuffed in the oven of your kitchen," Isabella said stiffly. She nodded. "The police are going to find out anyway. They're going to go through our personal affairs with a fine-tooth comb and if we don't get an expensive lawyer we might even be charged with murder."

"Nonsense. We didn't do it and we can prove it."

She gave him a gentle shove. "Go on, then. Tell her. It's not like it's anything to be ashamed of."

He stared at me, his lips a thin line. Finally, he burst out, "Very well, then. We were playing with our Echo."

This wasn't what she'd expected, so she raised an eyebrow. "Echo?"

"The Amazon gadget? You can ask it anything," Isabella said.

"Yeah, it's way cool. You can ask Alexa what the weather will be like, or to play a certain song, or to turn on the heating. Anything. It's fun."

"Who's Alexa?" she asked, still not following.

"She's the voice of the Echo," said Isabella.

"Like Apple has Siri?" Brainard added. He frowned. "I wonder why they're both women's voices."

"Women just have nicer voices," said Isabella.

"I'm sure that's not the reason."

"And I'm sure that it is."

"Um… How is this Echo thing providing you with an alibi?" Odelia asked.

"See, Brainard? Miss Poole is smart as a whip." She nudged him. "You tell her."

"No, you tell her. It was your idea, after all."

Isabella hooked her arm through her husband's and bit her lip. "The thing is… we were asking Alexa for… advice."

"Sexy positions," Brainard said gruffly, practicing his thousand-yard stare.

"And ordering sexy things online," his wife added.

"Spice up our love life. You should give it a try sometime, missy."

"Oh, I'm sure Miss Poole doesn't need her love life spiced up," Isabella said. She gave Odelia a smile. "When you're married for as long as we've been, you need all the spicing up you can get. You understand."

"Oh, sure," she said, a little flustered. "Yeah, I get it. Of course."

"And the good thing is that the police can check with Amazon. Everything you do on the Echo is recorded. So they can hear what we were up to."

"They can?" asked Brainard, his eyebrows rising precipitously.

"Oh, yes," she said, reddening slightly.

"Oh, my."

"Yes," she said with a sigh.

"Everything?"

"Every sound we made, honey."

"Oh, my God."

She bit her lip again. "So there you have it, Miss Poole. That's our alibi."

"Alexa."

She nodded. "I hope you'll be discreet about it. I'd hate for our friends and neighbors to find out about this. Or my sister."

"They'll know soon enough," said her husband. "Everybody talks, honey. Even the cops."

"Oh, well," she said, adjusting her dress. "It's not like it's a crime to have a good time. We are married, after all."

"And even if we weren't, there's no law against ordering edible lingerie."

"Brainard!" she whispered, tittering nervously.

"The Echo," Odelia said.

Isabella heaved a little sigh. "The Echo," she echoed.

Yep. Definitely one of the more interesting alibis.

CHAPTER 3

*W*e all stared at the newcomer, who sat casually licking his front paw.

"He's orange, just like you," Dooley whispered.

"I'm not orange, I'm blorange," I whispered back.

"What's the difference?" Brutus hissed.

"Blorange is a reddish orange with rose hues," I said.

They both stared at me, then at Diego, then back at me. "I don't see the difference," Brutus said.

"Well, there is a difference," I said haughtily. "Maybe you should have your eyes checked."

"My eyes are fine. You're orange, he's orange. It's the same color."

"It's not the same color!"

"No, you're right about that," Brutus admitted. "You're fat, he's thin."

"I'm not fat!"

Diego jumped up on the couch and casually stretched himself.

"Hey, that's my spot," I told Dooley.

"Tell him," Dooley said.

"Yeah, Max. You have to stand up for yourself," Brutus agreed. "Tell him that's your spot."

I hesitantly looked at Diego, then decided that he didn't look dangerous. Maybe he was even nice? I walked over, and said, "Hi, my name is Max, and I think you're in my spot."

He gave me a supercilious look, then placed his head on his paws and closed his eyes.

"Um... There are plenty of perfectly nice spots in this house, and you're welcome to them all," I said. "But this spot? Where you're lying now? That's, um... well, not to put too fine a point on it, but that spot is actually my spot, see?"

He opened his eyes again, and yawned. "What did you say your name was, brother?"

"Um, Max?"

He held up his paw. "Put it there."

I stared at his paw. "Put what there?"

"Give me some skin."

"Skin? What skin?"

"Press the flesh, dude."

"Press... the flesh? I... is that some kind of secret code?"

He sighed, then lowered his paw again. "Oh."

I stared at him. "Oh? What do you mean, Oh?"

"You're one of those."

"One of what?"

"A lame duck."

I gave a guffaw of incredulity. "For one thing, I'm not lame. And for another, I'm a cat, not a duck!"

"Whatever, dude," he said, going back to sleep.

This was too much. I tapped his shoulder and he opened his eyes again. "I'm sorry," I said. "Maybe I didn't make myself clear the first time, but this is my spot. You can't just waltz in here and take my spot. That's just... rude!"

"Hey, the blond babe said this was my house, so the way I see it? This spot is my spot. But, like you said, there's plenty of other spots in this place, bubba. Take your pick. And now if you could stop talking. Baby needz his ZZZs."

And he went right back to sleep!

I turned to face the others. I saw that Dooley was looking at me sadly, while Brutus was grinning like a fox. He seemed to be enjoying himself tremendously.

"Why don't you try singing it to him, 'bubba,'" Brutus suggested. "Or maybe you could send him a telegram and sign it, Max, heart heart heart."

"So what do you suggest?" I asked.

"I'd simply kick him off that couch. And if he doesn't like it, tough luck."

"Max doesn't kick cats off couches," Dooley said.

"Oh? And why is that?"

"Because Max doesn't believe in violence."

Brutus laughed. "This is just hilarious!"

"Hey, fatso," Diego said from the couch. "Zip it, will you? I'm trying to get some shut-eye here. Thanks, bubba."

Brutus made a strangled sound at the back of his throat. "Fatso?!" he finally managed. "Did you just call me fatso?"

"Yeah, do you see another fat cat in here?" Then he caught sight of me and grinned. "Oh, I see what you mean. Okay, what about this: Hey, black fatso. Shut it." He nodded at me. "I'll call you orange fatso from now on. That all right with you, bubba?"

"No, it's not all right with me!" I cried. "I'm not orange— I'm blorange!"

Diego rolled his eyes. "Tomato, tomahtoh. Blorange fatso, then, okay?"

"I'm not fat! I have big bones! It runs in my family!"

"And I'm not fat either," Brutus cried. "I'm muscular." He pounded his belly. "All muscle all the way. Not an ounce of fat."

"If it helps you sleep at night, go ahead and fool yourself," said Diego, stifling a yawn. "Hey, you, shorty," he said, addressing Dooley now.

Dooley pointed at himself. "Are you talking to me?"

"Yeah, I'm talking to you. Do you see another short cat in here? Can you tell me when lunch is served? I'm real particular about eating times."

Dooley was too stunned to respond. He just sat there, goggling.

Diego heaved out a sigh. "Short *and* dumb. What a combo. Maybe you can tell me, fat blorange cat. When do they serve lunch in this dump?"

"Max!" I cried, trembling with indignity now. "My name is Max!"

"Sure. Whatever you say, dude. So?" When I stared at him, he rolled his eyes again. "Geez Louise, do I have to spell it out for you? When. Do. They. Serve. Lunch. In. This. Dump? Never mind. I'll ask the blond bimbo when she comes back. I'll bet she's smarter than you bunch of chumps."

At this point, I, Brutus and Dooley all started yelling at the newcomer simultaneously. Unfortunately, he seemed oblivious, as he was staring past us in the direction of the French windows, which were open.

"Hey, gorgeous," Diego said, finally displacing himself and gracefully jumping down from the couch. "Where did you spring from? Heaven?"

I turned around to see who he was talking to, and saw that Harriet had entered the room. She was eyeing the newcomer curiously. "Who are you?"

Diego walked up to the white Persian and grinned. "Diego. I'm new in town. And you are…"

"Harriet."

"Lovely name for a lovely dame."

"So…" She gave me a confused look. "Do you live here now?"

"Yeah, Odelia adopted me. I'm here to stay, babe."

"Odelia adopted you?" Harriet asked.

"It's a long story. I belonged to this old babe, then she transferred me to this cop dude, and he decided to offload me so now I'm here."

"Oh, you poor thing," she said. "You've been through a lot, haven't you?"

He sighed. "Yeah, my life has not been a bed of roses, believe you me."

"Now that you're here, things are going to get better," she said.

"Now that you're here, I *know* things are gonna get better," he purred, waggling his whiskers seductively.

Oh, God. The cheesy lines just kept on coming! I was waiting for Harriet to finally catch on and put this guy in his place, but instead she was giving him the same look she used to give Brutus when he first arrived in Hampton Cove. Both Dooley and I glanced over at Brutus, who seemed to sit stunned, glued to the spot, eyes wide, his jaw on the floor.

"Sweetness!" Brutus finally managed. "My precious!"

Harriet looked up, and gave him a curt nod. "Hey, Brutus." But instead of going over to him and smothering him with revolting kisses, like she usually did, she stayed right where she was, checking out Diego.

Diego gave Brutus a smug smile, and asked Harriet, "Maybe you can show me around? Nobody has given me the grand tour of this place."

"They haven't?" She gave me an angry look. "Max! Where are your manners?"

"He called me fat," I said weakly.

"And orange," Dooley said, just as weakly.

"Hey, that's what buds do," said Diego. "Just some good-natured ribbing."

"Well, I'll show you around," said Harriet. "In fact why

don't I give you the tour of the town? Hampton Cove has a lot of great stuff to offer, and I can show you all of it."

"Oh, I don't doubt you can, babe," said Diego smoothly, unashamedly checking out Harriet's rear end and tail.

She giggled and tapped his shoulder. "You're funny."

"Thanks. I get that a lot. Especially from the ladies."

"You think I'm a lady?" she asked as she led him out the window.

"I think you're a babe. And a lady. A lady babe."

She giggled again. "Oh, you're just a regular riot, aren't you?"

"Sugar pie?" Brutus managed hoarsely. "Honeybunch?"

But Harriet was gone.

We sat there in stunned silence for the space of all of five seconds.

"What just happened?" I finally asked.

"I think Harriet likes the new cat," Dooley said sadly. He'd been through this before with Brutus, so he recognized the signs.

"This isn't happening," said Brutus. "Is it?"

He hadn't been through this before. In fact this was probably the first time he'd been thrown over by someone, so the experience was entirely new. I know I should have gloated, after what he'd put us through, but I honestly couldn't. The cat looked absolutely, positively sandbagged.

"It's happening," Dooley said, patting him on the back. "It just happened."

"Oh, God," he said, and I thought I heard an actual crack when the big lug's heart broke.

CHAPTER 4

*O*delia and Chase sat down for a cup of coffee at Cup o' Mika, the coffee shop across the street from the restaurant. The coroner was still checking the body, and Chief Alec was poking around the crime scene. Odelia had talked to some more people who worked in the restaurant and they'd all confirmed that Niklaus Skad hadn't made himself popular while he was filming the segment devoted to *Fry Me for an Oyster.*

"Looks like pretty much everyone had a motive to kill the guy," she said.

"Looks like. He wasn't exactly Mr. Popular," Chase agreed.

Both Chase and Uncle Alec had agreed that the crime scene was too gruesome for Odelia to see, so Chase had volunteered to keep her up to date.

"So tell me, what was so horrible?" she asked. "I mean, I've seen *Friday the Thirteenth*. I can handle blood and gore, Chase."

"Are you sure? Your mom once told me you can't watch a

scary movie without yelling to stop the movie, or disappearing into the kitchen when it gets really scary."

"Did Mom tell you that? She must have been talking about herself."

"I don't think so."

"Oh, all right. So I love scary movies but I can't stand the scary parts. So big deal. I'll bet there are lots of people who close their eyes or peek through their fingers when the girl is in the shower and the masked maniac sneaks in."

"That's such a cliché," he laughed. "I'm amazed they still keep doing scenes like that."

"Duh. Because they're classics? You have to have a shower scene."

"I thought that went out of style after *Psycho*. Hard to beat the master of suspense."

"Well, it still works, doesn't it? I mean, I can't watch a scene like that." She rolled her eyes. "Ugh. Now I gave myself away."

He laughed again. "You'd make a terrible killer. You'd crack during the first interview, and confess all of your crimes."

"I wouldn't even be interviewed. I've got one of those innocent faces. The police would take one look at me and would know I could never commit murder."

"That's true enough," he admitted. "You've got one of those honest, open faces. A face that displays everything that goes through your mind."

Oops. She hoped that the fact that she had a big secret to hide would never go through her head. Aaaand of course it just had. She tried to look innocent, opening her eyes wide and giving him her best, innocent smile.

"Now you look like you're about to lay an egg," he said skeptically.

"I do not!"

"Just kidding."

They sat there for a moment, enjoying a cup o' Joe and each other's company, and she wondered if there would ever be a repetition of the kiss he'd given her the other day in her parents' backyard. She'd kinda liked that kiss, and had hoped there were more where that one came from.

They locked eyes for a moment, and she wondered if he could read that particular thought on her face. He gave her a small smile, and she returned it.

"So, the crime scene," he said finally, ending their little moment.

"Yes, the crime scene. Tell me all about it. In gruesome detail."

"Though not too gruesome. Well, apparently the killer somehow managed to stuff the body of our celebrity chef into the oven and—"

"Wait, stuff him in the oven? How big is this oven?"

"Big enough to roast a body, which is what they did."

"Niklaus Skad was roasted?"

"Yes, roasted like a pig. Or a duck. Or whatever you want to roast."

"Eww. Now I don't want to roast anything."

"Yeah, me neither," he admitted.

"At least did they kill him first before roasting him?"

Chase lifted his massive shoulders in a shrug. "Dunno. It's up to Abe to figure that out."

Abe Cornwall was the county coroner and a very able professional. If anyone could figure out what had killed the celebrity chef, it was him.

"I'd say he's got his work cut out for him," Chase continued. "The body was completely unrecognizable. Had been simmering all night."

Odelia shivered in spite of herself. Now here was one of those moments she wanted to close her eyes and then peek at

31

the screen from between her fingers. "Yuck." Her eyes widened. "You don't think they shoved him in there alive, do you? That would be a terrible way to go."

"Abe doesn't think so. If that were the case there would have been claw marks or signs that he'd tried to escape. Most likely scenario is that he was knocked out—either dead or unconscious—before being cooked."

"So do you and Uncle Alec have any suspects?"

"Plenty. There's the owners of the restaurant, who were afraid to lose their business if Niklaus labeled them incompetent. There's the chef, who seemed to be the one Niklaus singled out for abuse the most. And then there's the other staff, who clearly all hated Niklaus and wanted him gone."

"I talked to the Stowes. They have an alibi."

She explained to him about the Echo, and Chase had to laugh.

"That must be one of the most original alibis I've ever heard. Oh, and we'll definitely check if it's true."

"I'll bet you will," she said with a grin.

"Don't worry. I'll give you the PG-13 version," he said.

"Hey! I may be scared of scary movies, but I'm old enough to hear all the saucy bits they ordered on Amazon!"

His grin spread. "I'll bet you're dying to find out."

"So I can order some of that stuff myself? In your dreams, buddy."

"You're right about that," he said, and his look gave her an instant hot flash. Oh, boy. Was she in trouble or not? "Anyway," he continued. "Next on our list is Hendrik Serarols, who's pulled a disappearing act."

"Have you tried his house?"

"Apartment. Yes, a couple of unis went by his place. Nobody home."

"Unis?"

"Uniformed officers. Sorry. Force of habit."

Just then, Odelia's phone rang and she saw that it was her grandmother. "I have to take this. It's Gran."

"I'll get us another round, shall I?" he suggested, and disappeared inside.

"Hey, Gran. What's up?"

"Odelia, honey, the strangest thing has happened. I was opening a present I got from Leo and—"

"Who's Leo?"

"Oh, just a guy I'm seeing."

"You're seeing a guy?"

"Yes, I'm seeing a guy. Can't I see a guy? You're seeing a guy."

"I'm not seeing a guy."

"I saw you kissing that cop."

"That was... nothing."

"If that was nothing I'd like to see what something looks like."

She pressed her fingers to her brow. "So you were opening Leo's present?"

"Yeah, a nice cashmere sweater. Not sure why he would buy me a cashmere sweater in the summer, unless it's to tell me he wants me to cover up more, but from the way he's all over me every time we go out I can tell that's not it. So that's a mixed message right there. Anyway, I guess there's no accounting for taste." She paused. "What was I talking about?"

"You opened the present and something strange happened?"

"That's right. There was a note inside the sweater."

"A note? What note?"

"I didn't see it at first. I just saw it when I cut off the label. I always cut off the label. It just pricks my skin. I hate it. Don't you hate it? They should make it softer. Like velvety soft. I've got delicate skin, so—"

"Gran..."

"So I cut off the label and there it was, neatly folded inside the label, a little note. I had to put on my glasses to read it."

"What did it say?"

"Wait—where are my glasses? They keep stealing them from me. Oh, they're on top of my head. Hey, not so fast! Sit down and wait. The doctor will be with you soon!"

Gran was obviously at work, at Dad's doctor's office, bullying the patients into submission as usual. "So what does the label say?"

"Hold your horses. Not so fast. Lemme just put these on and... 'WE PRISONERS! PLEASE HELP PLEASE!' Notice how it says Please twice? Whoever wrote this has got good manners. Want me to read it again?"

"No, I think I got it," she said, holding the phone away from her ear. Gran had shouted the message so loud her eardrum was still buzzing. She watched as three cats came trudging up to her. They were Max, Dooley and Brutus, and they looked like they had some very important news to impart. "Is it all right if I drop by later? I'd like to take a closer look at this note."

"Sure thing, honey. I'll be here all day. Sit down, buddy—this is my final warning! SIT! Like I said, I'll be here all day, helping these nice people."

Odelia disconnected, and wondered what this was all about. She'd heard about people finding messages in their clothes or household devices. Stuff made in developing countries, where working conditions were appalling. This was probably such a case. It just hurt her heart when she heard stories like that.

"Hey, you guys," she said, lowering her head to the three cats. "Any news?"

"Yes," Max said. "The new cat? Diego? He's got to go. He's bad news."

CHAPTER 5

"That cat's got to go," I repeated, in case Odelia hadn't heard me the first time.

"Yeah, he's a terrible, horrible animal," Dooley chimed in.

"He took Harriet away from me," Brutus said. "Just like that."

"Hold it, you guys," said Odelia, laughing. "What are you saying? That you don't like Diego?"

"That's exactly what we're saying," I said. "He called me fat and orange."

"And he called me short and dumb," said Dooley.

"And he put the moves on Harriet," Brutus finished our lament.

"Oh, and don't forget he called you fat, too," Dooley said.

"She doesn't have to know that," Brutus said in a low voice. "I may have gained some weight, but not much. And I still work out every day. I climbed a tree just this morning. And I got down all on my own, too."

"Look, you'll just have to learn to get along," Odelia said. "You can't expect me to kick out Diego. I just told Chase I'd take care of him."

"You can put him up for adoption," I suggested. "I bet there are plenty of people out there who'd love to take him in."

"Unless they have other cats—Diego doesn't play nice with others," Dooley said.

"He doesn't play nice with males. He's fine with females," said Brutus.

"A little too nice," Dooley added.

Odelia shook her head. "What can I say?"

"That you'll kick him out?" I asked hopefully.

"I can't do that, Max. I'm afraid Diego is here to stay."

Dooley, Brutus and I voiced our disagreement loud and clear, but to no avail. Apparently Odelia was set on keeping this Diego in our lives, whether we liked it or not. Just then, Chase returned, and Odelia immediately shut up.

Chase laughed. "You know? It almost looked like you were talking to those cats of yours. It's the funniest thing."

She gave him a tight smile. "Sometimes I almost feel like I know what they're trying to say."

He studied us. "So what are they saying?"

"I'm not sure, but I think it might have something to do with that cat of yours."

"Diego? What about him?"

"I think they don't like him very much."

He laughed again. "That's ridiculous. They're cats. There's no question of liking each other. They just act on instinct." It was obvious he'd never given a moment's thought to the fact that cats might have feelings, too. Just like humans. And that maybe some of us were nicer than others.

"Cats are a lot more like humans than you might think," Odelia said. "They have likes and dislikes, just like we do."

"Nonsense. This has got nothing to do with 'feelings.' This is about territory. Max is probably upset that a new cat has

36

arrived and he's going to have to share his space, his food and his litter box."

I goggled at the man. I hadn't thought about that. Share my food? And, even worse, share my litter box? No way! "Odelia! I can't share my litter box! That's my litter box! Diego can't go doo-doo in my litter box! That's just... wrong!"

She ignored me, and asked Chase, "What do you know about Diego?"

He shrugged. "He's a cat, Odelia. What's there to know?"

"I mean, about his past, his parentage, his medical history?"

"I'd have to ask Mom, but as far as I know she got him off the street."

"So he's a street cat. Did she give him his shots? Is he fixed?"

"I have absolutely no idea."

She nodded. "I'll take him to the vet tomorrow. Have him checked."

"Of course. And I'll pay for it. Look, I'm sure Max and Diego will get along fine. They just have to get used to each other. I wouldn't worry about it if I were you."

"Well, I do worry about it. If I'm going to take Diego into my home, I need to know who I'm dealing with."

Well spoken, I thought, and I was cheering for her. Maybe this Diego had a violent past, or some other deep, dark secret that he was hiding. Maybe he was like those adopted kids that turn out to be horrible serial killers. I'd seen the movies. I knew it was a thing.

"Look, if you don't want him, I can always take him back," Chase offered.

I was practically yipping now, hoping Odelia would take him up on this wonderful offer. This was her chance to get rid of the pest!

"No, that's all right," she said, much to my horrified surprise. She stroked my back. "Max will just have to get used to having a new friend. I know it took him a while to get used to having Brutus around, and now look at them. They're like buddies."

Odelia and Chase looked down at Brutus and me, sitting side by side, like a couple of chumps. "I think they're talking about us, Max," Brutus said.

"Yeah, they seem to think we're best buds or something."

Brutus snorted. "As if."

"Yeah—how ridiculous, huh? Humans are clueless."

We shared a quick look, then Brutus said, "I liked how you stood up to Diego, by the way. That took guts, Max. I've got to hand it to you. You defended hearth and home from that intruder—just like you used to do with me."

"I know, right? I felt like I had to take a firm line with the cat. And you were great, too. The way you put him in his place? Way to go, Brutus."

"Thanks. I mean, it's not my home to defend, but still. He was way out of line."

"Well, it is your home now, in a way," I said.

"You really mean that, Max?"

"Sure. *Mi casa es su casa* and all that, right?"

"Aww. That's awfully nice of you."

"Don't mention it. I feel like we have to stick together and make a stand."

"Yeah. Let's put our differences aside and get rid of the new cat."

"What about me?" Dooley asked. "Is *su casa mi casa* too, Max?"

"Of course, buddy! You're my best friend."

"Thanks, Max. I love you, too."

Brutus eyed us with a strange look on his face. Then he held out his paw. "Put it there, pals."

I put it there, and so did Dooley.

"Buds?" asked Brutus.

"Buds," I said.

"I think they're actually talking to each other," Chase said. "It's way cute."

"They are talking to each other," Odelia assured him. "Cats can communicate."

"So, do you have any idea what they're saying?" he asked.

"Not a clue," she said, and gave us a wink.

CHAPTER 6

*J*ust when their order arrived—an espresso for Chase and a latte for Odelia—Chase got a call from Chief Alec.

"Uh-oh," he said, disconnecting. "Looks like I gotta run. The Chief managed to locate Serarols."

"The chef?"

"He's down at the station now, and he's asked me to be there when he questions him."

"Just go. I'll take care of your espresso."

He grinned. "I'm sure you will." He took the espresso and downed it in one gulp. "Just so happens I love espressos, though, so tough luck."

"You'll keep me in the loop, right?"

"Sure." He got up and threw a few bills on the table. "Thanks for the chat—and the update on the world of cats. It was fun—and instructional."

"See you later, Chase."

She watched him leave, and noticed not for the first time that he moved with a catlike grace. Like a tiger. Or a panther. It also occurred to her he was a lot more dangerous than she thought when he first just moved into town. She'd never figured she'd ever fall for the cop, and now she found that he was on her mind a lot more than she knew how to handle.

She looked down, and saw that Max, Dooley and Brutus had left. She hated to disappoint them, but she'd already agreed to take Diego in, and she couldn't go back on her word now. She was pretty sure it would be fine. When Brutus just arrived, Max and Dooley had been equally distraught. And look at them now. They were like buddies these days.

She took a sip of her latte and thought about the case. With so many suspects, it was going to be a matter of deciding who had most to gain from the celebrity chef's murder. And who'd been in the position to carry out the murder. She imagined it would have had to be a person with considerable physical strength, as it was a tough feat to hoist the chef into the oven.

She looked out across the street at the restaurant, and saw a woman sashay in her direction. She recognized her from several covers of *Star Magazine*. Cybil Truscott, the soon-to-be ex-wife of Niklaus Skad. And as luck would have it, she was heading straight for the coffee shop.

The woman, large sunglasses on her nose, her hair a lustrous shiny red, her skin a milky white and dressed in designer threads, was carrying three shopping bags in each hand, all from luxury boutiques. It was obvious she'd just gone on a shopping spree. To celebrate the death of her husband?

Cybil took a seat at the next table, and Odelia leaned over. "Excuse me, but aren't you Cybil Truscott?"

The woman smiled, and took off her sunglasses, shaking out her gorgeous mane of red curls. "Yes, I am. And you are?"

"Odelia Poole. I'm a reporter for the Hampton Cove Gazette."

The woman's smile widened. "Ooh, I love reporters. And they love me."

Of course they did. Ever since Cybil got married to Niklaus Skad, she'd been tabloid fodder, her pictures appearing on more covers than any other starlet or socialite or celebrity wannabe. She'd been a cocktail waitress before she met Niklaus, and now she wasn't just famous, she stood to gain a substantial fortune after the death of her husband.

"My condolences," she said now. "I just heard about your husband."

"Yes, shocking, isn't it?" She glanced across the street. "And that's where it happened. Such a sad ending for such a brilliant man. Then again, there is a certain poetic justice in the fact that he would die in the oven of one of the restaurants he was singling out for his notorious brand of abuse."

"I didn't know you were in town," Odelia said.

"Yes, I'm on vacation. I'm staying at the Hampton Springs Hotel."

"Did you know your husband would be in town?"

"I had no idea! Of course we hadn't been in touch lately. We only communicated through our lawyers. Ever since I filed for divorce Niklaus broke off all relations."

Which stood to reason. She had accused him in several TV interviews of domestic violence and of assaulting her. There were even rumors of him forcing her into accepting a trio with the housekeeper. Odelia had the impression a lot of the stories Cybil had dished were simply a way to get as much out of the divorce as possible. Hoping her famous husband would pay her a large sum of money just to shut her up.

"So you didn't see him last night?" she asked innocently.

The woman threw her head back and laughed. "Oh, honey, I have to hand it to you. You may be writing for some local rag, but you're good at what you do. You're trying to figure out if I killed my husband, aren't you?"

"Well, you do have a solid motive," she admitted.

Cybil gave her a shrewd look. "I know what you're thinking. Niklaus was never going to allow me the divorce settlement I was aiming for. Why not kill the man instead and take it all? And you're right. With him gone, I stand to inherit his entire fortune. The houses in New York, Vail, Los Angeles, Paris, London and Antibes. The business empire he built. The royalties to his bestselling books. The cars, the yachts, the private jet... You name it, I will get it now. But did I kill him? Of course not. I may be a money-grubbing social climber, like the papers will undoubtedly point out—and Niklaus's friends and ex-wives have done for years—but I'm not a murderer. Besides, I have one of those things you need when someone is killed. What's it called? An amoeba?"

"An alibi?"

She snapped her fingers. "That's it. I've got me one of those. Ironclad one, too."

"And would you care to share your alibi with me?"

She laughed again. "Oh, darling. You're good, but not that good. I think I'll keep that for the police. If or when they decide to haul me in for questioning."

"I work with the police, actually. My uncle is Chief of Police."

"I see. So that's why you're so nosy. And here I thought you were going to write a nice big front-page article about me." She pouted.

"I will write a nice big article about you," Odelia promised.

"But only if I tell you about my alibi, right?"

She smiled. "I'll find out soon enough anyway."

"From your uncle. I see." She waved an airy hand. "Just ask the pool boy at the Hampton Springs Hotel. He'll tell you all you need to know. With all the saucy details you gossip hounds are so crazy about."

"Thanks," she said. "I will talk to him."

Cybil winked. "There's even pictures. Lots and lots of them. And video." Then she looked across the street at the yellow-and-black crime scene tape and sobered. "I did like him once upon a time, you know. Niklaus? He was a vulgar man with a cruel streak, but he had passion. Lots of passion, if you know what I mean."

Odelia had an idea she knew exactly what the woman meant. She didn't want to know, though. She wasn't that kind of reporter.

"When we first got together we went at it like bunny rabbits." She seemed to shake herself, and gave a slight shrug. "But passion fades, and money doesn't, so…"

"So you decided to cash in your chips before he did?"

"You are smart. What did you say your name was?"

"Odelia Poole."

The woman took out her smartphone, and before Odelia could stop her had snapped a selfie of the two of them together. She then flicked her long fingernails across the screen for a few seconds and gave a tiny smile. "Done and done," she said, holding up her phone for Odelia to read.

"Chatting with Odelia Poole, who's no fool!" she read. "Nice."

"You don't have to thank me when the endorsement deals start rolling in, darling. Call it giving something back to the community. After all, I can afford it."

Odelia left the coffee shop feeling a little queasy. She didn't know whether Cybil Truscott was a murderer or not, but she was sure she was not a very nice person.

CHAPTER 7

*B*rutus went home to check up on Harriet. He'd decided that the best way to deal with this upstart was to cramp his style—make sure Harriet was never alone with him. It was a great idea. Problem was, Harriet had promised to show Diego the town, so by now they could be anywhere.

Dooley and I decided to check out the restaurant. Even though we were a little bit annoyed with Odelia right now, for saddling us up with Diego, we couldn't let her down. She relied on us to gather valuable information about this murder and we felt we had to help her get it.

"You know, if we catch the killer we could tell Odelia we're only going to reveal the name if she promises to show Diego the door," Dooley suggested.

"We can't do that, Dooley," I said. "That wouldn't be right."

"Is it right she foisted that orange cat on us? I mean—just saying."

"We have to make it clear to her what kind of cat Diego

really is. The moment she knows him like we do, she won't hesitate to kick him out."

"I wouldn't be too sure about that."

"Well, I am sure. I trust Odelia. She's always come through for us, and I'm sure she will come through for us now."

We'd arrived in the back alley behind the restaurant, hoping to meet a kindred spirit—a fellow feline. We strode over to the dumpster that was parked next to the kitchen entrance and saw that we were right on the money: someone had placed a bowl of milk next to the dumpster, and another bowl with what looked like chicken nuggets.

"Yum," Dooley said, licking his lips. How that cat manages to stay so thin, I don't know. He never stops eating.

"Don't touch that, Dooley," I told him. "That's not yours."

"It's on public property, which makes it everyone's, including mine."

"You can't just go digging into another cat's bowl. That would make you just as bad as Diego."

Dooley started. "Are you comparing me to Diego? That's mean, Max."

"I'm sorry, but it's true. This bowl belongs to someone, and that someone isn't you."

We stared around, hoping to find this mysterious some-one. As far as I could see, there was no one around. "Do you think Harriet is going to fall for Diego?" Dooley wanted to know.

"I don't think so. She's smarter than that."

"She wasn't smart enough not to fall for Brutus."

"Well, Brutus isn't Diego. Diego seems to be way worse than Brutus."

"They're pretty much the same, Max. Brutus is just being nice to us now that he needs us. The moment Diego is gone, he'll be back to his mean old ways."

That was a scenario I hadn't considered. "Do you think so?"

"I know so. They're exactly the same, Brutus and Diego. Big bad bullies."

"Don't you think Brutus has changed?"

"No way. Bullies don't change. If anything they just get meaner and nastier as they get older. I'm telling you, Brutus is just acting like he likes us. Deep down he still hates us."

"What are you guys talking about?"

I turned around, and saw we'd been joined by a smallish black cat, who sat licking her fur while keeping a keen eye on us and the two bowls. I had no idea where she'd come from. One moment she wasn't there, the next she was. Like magic.

"Um, hi," I said. "I'm Max, and this is Dooley."

"We were talking about another cat," Dooley said. "A bully."

"Two bullies, actually," I said.

The black cat nodded sagely. "Trust me, I know all about bullies. We had one in here this past week. Nastiest bully I've ever seen. Drove everyone to tears."

"You mean Niklaus Skad? The celebrity chef?" I asked.

"That's the one. Yelling and screaming all day long. Nasty brute."

"You do know that he was murdered, right?" asked Dooley.

"Oh, sure. It's the talk of the neighborhood. We were all rooting for this Skad guy to leave soon and take his brand of foul abuse along with him."

"So do you have any idea who killed him?" I asked.

She shook her head. "No idea. I wasn't here last night. A buddy of mine was, though. He said there was a car parked out back, right next to that dumpster. A very expensive car."

"What kind of car?" I asked.

She laughed. "You have to excuse me. I don't know

anything about cars. My buddy said it was a Tesla?" She laughed again. "He said it looked just like my fur. Obsidian black, he calls it. Whatever that is."

"A Tesla is an electric car," I said. "There aren't that many of those around. Did your buddy get a license plate number?"

"Oh, no, nothing like that. In fact Fred was just passing by the restaurant—that's his name: Fred—though I have a sneaking suspicion he was looking for me. He doesn't want to admit it but I think Fred likes me."

"That's nice," I said, not interested in the cat's romantic proclivities. "So about that Tesla—did Fred see a driver? Anyone hanging around?"

"Nope. When he told me I figured it probably belonged to Niklaus Skad. He was always arriving in fancy rides. Though he seemed to have a penchant for sports cars." She pointed to a BMW Roadster that was parked halfway down the alley. "That's his car right there. He must have arrived and never left."

Dooley and I stared blankly at the BMW, then my mind turned back to the Tesla. It was significant, and I vowed to tell Odelia first chance I got.

"Oh, my name is Montserrat, by the way," the black cat said.

"Is that your food, Montserrat?" Dooley asked, pointing at the bowl.

"Dooley!" I hissed.

"What? Just asking."

Montserrat giggled. "No, that's not my food, silly. Erin put that out here for the strays. I have my bowl inside. Erin's taken a liking to me. She works here and makes sure all my needs are met." She sighed. "I'm sure lucky with her. Do you guys have humans or are you just a couple of strays?"

"I'm sorry," I said, indignant. "I'm not a stray. Can't you tell?"

She studied me for a moment. "You look very well fed for a stray. You, on the other hand," she added, turning to Dooley, "I had pegged as a stray from the moment I saw you. You look… skinny, if you know what I mean. As if you're gonna die from starvation any second. Actually, if you want, you can eat from the public bowl. Erin put it there for strays like you."

Dooley gaped at her. "I look like I'm about to die?"

"Yeah, you do, actually," she confirmed. "So better tuck in, little buddy. Eat your fill before it's too late. I think Erin even left some fish in there. Go on, then. Don't be shy."

"Yeah, Dooley," I said. "Tuck in. Don't be shy."

But Dooley looked crushed. "I suddenly lost my appetite."

"Actually we both belong to a human," I told Montserrat. "My human is Odelia Poole? The reporter? And Dooley's human is Odelia's grandmother."

"Oh, so you do have a human," said Montserrat. "Sorry about that, little buddy. You have to tell her to feed you better. You're just skin and bones."

As we left the alley, Dooley was completely discombobulated.

"Do I really look that bad, Max?" he asked.

"You look fine to me, Dooley."

"But Montserrat said I look like I'm about to die."

"I'm sure she was exaggerating."

"Maybe I've got some kind of wasting disease. Maybe I'm sick and I don't even know it!"

"You're not sick. You're just skinny. Some cats are skinny, others are big-boned, like me. It's body type, that's all. Nothing to worry about."

"But I do worry, Max." He shook his head. "I should see a doctor."

"I'm sure you're fine," I repeated. "So what about that Tesla, huh? Great clue. I can't wait to tell Odelia."

"Maybe I should go see Tex. He's a doctor, right?"

"Tex is a doctor for humans. You need an animal doctor."

He gave me a look of panic. "I do?"

"No, I mean, if you WERE sick, which you're NOT, you would have to see a vet. But since you're NOT sick, you DON'T, if you see what I mean." I tried to make my meaning perfectly clear, but Dooley wasn't having any of it.

"You just said I needed to see an animal doctor, Max. Don't try to deny it."

"I'm not denying anything!"

"Yes, you are." He gave me a penetrating look. "How long have you known, Max? Who else knows? Does Odelia know?"

"Know what?"

"That I'm dying!"

"You're not dying!"

"You're all keeping the truth from me. This is a conspiracy!"

Oh, crap. Thank you, Montserrat, I thought. This was just like that time Dooley thought he was a pedigree cat that a famous person had abandoned. For weeks he hounded us with his stories of how Mariah Carey or Katy Perry would come looking for him and how there would be a touching reunion. No matter what I said, he didn't believe me. This was going to be the exact same thing, I just knew it.

"You're not dying."

"So you say."

"Yes, because I know."

"How? You're not a doctor."

"I know because you look just fine."

"I'm skin and bone!"

"You've always been skin and bone!"

"So maybe I've always been sick!"

Yep. This was going to be a long couple of weeks.

CHAPTER 8

*O*delia walked into her dad's doctor's office. Tex
Poole was Hampton Cove's resident general practi-
tioner. He was a gregarious man, and good at what he did, so
his waiting room was always full. He was one of the last of
his kind, as all around Hampton Cove clinics had sprung up,
with several doctors combining their skills to offer a full-
service medical package. And then there were the concierge
doctors, catering to the wealthy, of which the Hamptons
boasted more than a few. Tex was an old-fashioned doctor,
though, who treated old and young, rich and poor, men or
women, of any ailments that might have befallen them.

Odelia found her grandmother presiding over the waiting
room as usual, talking on the phone and jotting down a name
in the big appointment book. What wasn't usual was that
there was a man seated next to her, a vacuous look on his
face, his hand on Gran's shoulder, and his shirt unbuttoned.

He was an older man that she didn't recognize, with
wrinkled features, bushy brows, a full head of white hair, and
quite a lot of hair on his chest as well.

She stared at the man, pulling up short the moment she stepped inside.

"Please don't be tardy, Mrs. Mueller," Gran was saying. "Doctor Poole doesn't appreciate tardiness. If you're tardy you will have to reschedule." She hung up and her face creased into a thousand wrinkles the moment her gaze landed on her granddaughter. "Odelia, honey. Am I glad to see you."

"Um, Gran," she said, hesitantly approaching the desk. "There's a man next to you."

"Oh, this is Leo. I told you about Leo, didn't I? He's the one that gave me the cashmere sweater. Leo, say hi to my granddaughter Odelia."

"Hi," said Leo, and lapsed into silence once more.

"Leo's not a talker," said Gran. "But he makes up for it with his other skills," she added with a cheeky wink.

"Thanks, Gran. Um, do you mind me asking why Leo is naked?"

Gran eyed her boyfriend for a moment. "Naked? What are you talking about? I don't see where he's naked. He's all dressed up as far as I can see."

"His shirt is unbuttoned. I don't think Dad would approve."

"Leo gets hot," said Gran. "He's one of those men that get hot. So he likes to unbutton his shirt, so what?"

"What are the patients going to think?" she asked.

"They can think whatever they want. When you get to my age you stop caring what people think. It's one of the few blessings of being old."

Odelia squinched her eyes closed. "Leo?"

The old guy looked up. "Mh?"

"Could you please button up your shirt? And could you please remove your arm from my grandmother's shoulder? This is a doctor's office, not a bar. Thank you," she added when Leo complied. Of course, to button up his shirt, he had to remove his arm from Gran's shoulder. The minute he'd accomplished this task, the arm was right back, and Gran didn't seem to mind one bit. It was... awkward.

"What?" Gran asked. "Leo's a very physical man. I like it."

"Well, maybe you should get physical on your own time," she said. "Not when you're working."

"Hey, who died and made you boss? Show a little respect for your grandmother. I had men's arms around me when you weren't even born."

"Gran, it just... isn't proper," she said, uttering words she'd never thought she'd speak to her grandmother, or to anyone else for that matter.

"Oh, all right," said Gran, removing Leo's arm. "But I'm only doing it as a favor to you," she said. When Leo made a protesting sound, she patted his hand. "I'm off at three, honey. Come and see me then, all right?"

Leo left the office, giving Odelia a very unfriendly glance.

"I don't think Leo likes me," Odelia said once he'd left.

"Do you think?"

"I'm sorry, Gran. But I think you can do better than... that."

"Honey, when you're as old as I am you can't take any chances. When you're lucky enough to get hold of a live one you better hang on. You never know when he's gonna die on you. Speaking of dying, did you hear about that celebrity chef that got cooked in his own oven?"

"Yes, I'm on the case."

"And so is Chase, right?" she asked, giving her a saucy wink.

"Yes," she admitted, staunchly ignoring the wink.

"I like that man. Too bad he's into you or else I'd have gone after him myself."

"Yes. You've made that abundantly clear, Gran," she said. "So what's this about a note in your sweater?"

Gran dumped the sweater on the counter. "This is the sweater," she said, then plunked down a little piece of paper. "And here is the note. I told Leo and he was so surprised he spoke a complete sentence. First time I've heard more coming out of that man's mouth than grunts and moans. Heh heh heh."

She held up a hand. "Please, Gran. I don't need to hear the details."

"Why not? You might learn a thing or two. Have you and that cop done it already?"

She cast a quick glance at the two women and one man who sat patiently waiting for her dad to call them in. The women were studiously poring over copies of *Woman's Day* and *Family Circle* while the man pretended to read *Field and Stream*. She knew they were hanging on her and Gran's every word, though.

She lowered her voice. "That's none of your business, Gran!"

Gran arched a finely penciled eyebrow. "Oh? You come in here bitching and moaning about Leo's buttons and I can't even ask you a simple question?"

"That's different. I don't..." She dropped her voice even more. "I don't do it where the whole town can see us."

Gran's lips curled into a knowing smile. "So you didn't do it, huh? Thought as much. Better get a move on, girlfriend. A man like Chase won't wait around forever. And you know what they say about women that don't put out."

"No, I don't," she said between clenched teeth. "And I don't care."

"They're prudes. And you don't want to be a prude. That's the curse of death right there. You'll never date in this town again. Only guys who'll still want you are idiots, and you don't want them mucking up the Poole bloodline."

"Gran! That's so wrong on so many levels I don't even… Ugh."

"Right or wrong, you better take a page out of my book, honey, or else Chase will chase after some other chick. Now, where were we? Oh, right. The note."

Odelia, shaking her head, picked up the note. Her grandmother was right. It said, 'WE PRISONERS! PLEASE HELP PLEASE!' It was a small piece of paper, and the writing was shaky, as if whoever had written it was under great duress.

She turned it over. There was nothing on the other side, and nothing whatsoever to indicate where it had come from. No identification, no clue as to where this person was being held prisoner or when the note was written.

"I think it's from Russia," said Gran. "Stalin's got all those prison camps over there? In Siberia? One of 'em prisoners must have smuggled out this sweater."

"So how did the sweater get here? Besides, they don't have prison camps in Russia anymore, Gran. They went out of fashion when Stalin died, remember? In the nineteen-fifties?"

"So who wrote it then, Little Miss Know-It-All?"

"Lemme see that sweater." She studied the label. Ziv Riding. "Wow. Pretty expensive."

Grandma beamed. "I told you. Leo's into me."

"Leo must be into you a lot. This is Ziv Riding."

"Is he famous or something?"

"Only one of the hottest designers working right now. He shot to the top out of nowhere, and he's been the star of New York Fashion Week three years in a row. Are you sure Leo didn't steal this from someplace?"

Gran planted her hand on her hip. "Hey. Don't insult my Leo. I'll have you know the guy is loaded."

She gave Gran a crooked smile. "I saw that."

"Moneywise, smartass. Though you're right. The guy is packing, if you know what I mean."

She raised her eyes heavenward. "I don't think I want to know."

She studied the sweater some more. Gran had snipped off the wash care label, which had contained the note. So whoever had made this sweater had wanted to cry out for help, and make sure the message went out. But then why hadn't they also added instructions for whoever found the message? Weird. She decided it wasn't really worth looking into. She knew that top designers like Ziv Riding had all of their clothes made in countries like Bangladesh or India or the Philippines. So whoever had left this desperate message was way out of reach.

"This is just so horrible," she said, as she pictured a woman or man or even a child chained down in some sweatshop on the other side of the world, having to make these clothes so they could be bought by rich Westerners, making the designers who exploited these workers even richer.

"Yeah, Ziv Riding is a douche."

"Well, maybe he doesn't even know his clothes are made in these sweatshops. A lot of times they just hand over production to a company."

"Then they should make sure those companies don't use sweatshops."

She was right, of course. Then again, there wasn't much she could do about that from where she stood. So she handed the note back to her grandmother, along with the sweater. "Where did Leo buy this?"

"In one of the boutiques on Main Street. So are you going to expose this Ziv Riding? Are you going to write a tell-all exposé about the guy?"

She shook her head. "I can't, Gran. I can't accuse him of anything without more information."

"So gather more information. You're a reporter. That's your job."

"I'm just a small-town reporter. I don't write stories like this. I write about a new shop opening on Main Street. Or that traffic lights were out again at the intersection. Or about the council meeting. I don't expose international scandals."

"Well, I think you should." Gran held up the note. "This is an outrage. Those poor people wrote this note hoping someone would find it. Someone with the guts to stand up to people like Riding. Someone who'd save them."

She held up her hands. "Well, that person isn't me."

"Wimp," Gran muttered, dumping the sweater behind the counter.

"Gee, thanks, Gran. I don't see you climbing the barricades or picketing outside Ziv Riding's office."

"Well, maybe I will," said Gran. "Maybe me and Leo will do just that."

Sure. That would make Ziv Riding quake in his designer boots. Gran and Leo picketing his office. When they weren't too busy smooching.

CHAPTER 9

*D*ooley and I passed into the offices of the Hampton Cove Gazette. It wasn't a difficult feat as the editor kept the door unlocked, in case a member of the public decided to step in and regale him with some fresh story or offer comment on an article he'd written. Dan is a fixture in Hampton Cove, and you can't miss him. He's a smallish man with a big, white beard and lots of laugh wrinkles around his eyes. These days he mainly takes care of the business side of running a paper and lets Odelia write the articles.

We passed by Dan's office, where the editor spent most of his days, and on to Odelia's, smaller office, right next to his. She was at her desk, pounding away at an article, presumably about the murder. In spite of what you might think, murders rarely happen in Hampton Cove, so when one does happen, it's a big deal.

"Hey, guys," she said as we rubbed against her leg. She picked me up and put me on her desk. I proceeded to lie down on her keyboard, easily the best spot in the house as it gets most of Odelia's attention.

She gently gave me a push, and I reluctantly scooted over, idly playing with her mouse until she took it away from me and placed it out of reach. Humans. Never any fun.

"So we discovered a clue," I said.

"And I discovered that I'm about to die," Dooley said morosely.

She stared from me to Dooley, clearly not sure where to begin, so I decided to help her out. "Montserrat, the cat that belongs to Erin Coka, told us her friend Fred saw a black Tesla parked in the alley behind the restaurant last night. And she's sure it doesn't belong to the owners of the place or anyone who works there."

"I'm wasting away," Dooley announced.

"So whoever killed Niklaus Skad drives an obsidian black Tesla," I said. "Don't thank us, thank Montserrat. And Fred."

"It must be cancer," Dooley continued. "What else could it be?"

"Um..." Odelia said. "First of all, thanks for the Tesla thing? Secondly, why do you think you're dying, Dooley?"

"It's Montserrat's fault," I told her. "She may be great at ferreting out crucial information like the killer's ride, but she sucks at social niceties. Like, she told me I was fat? And then she went and said Dooley must be sick he's so thin. I mean, who does that, right?"

"Montserrat is right. I am freakishly thin," Dooley said.

"She didn't say you were freakishly thin," I said. "She said you looked like a stray and that your human probably doesn't feed you enough. There's a difference."

"How is that different? She thought I was dying."

"She didn't think he was dying," I told Odelia. "just that he's thin."

Odelia looked worried now. "Doesn't Gran feed you enough?"

"Actually Gran doesn't feed me anything," Dooley said.

NIC SAINT

"Omigod, she doesn't?"

"No, your mom feeds me. Gran forgets, so Marge took over years ago. She feeds Harriet and me, though Harriet gets special treatment, on account of her fur. She gets something that's guaranteed to put the shine in a Persian's fur."

"So why is it this…"

"Montserrat," I said helpfully.

"This Montserrat thinks you're too thin?"

"Because she's flaky," I said.

"Because she sees a lot of strays, and she said I look like one."

"You don't look like a stray, Dooley," Odelia said softly, picking up Dooley and depositing him right next to me. "You look like a very healthy, very happy cat."

"You think so?" he asked hesitantly.

"Sure. I don't think there's anything wrong with you. You're just thin, but that's body type for you. Just like Max here is full-figured."

"I prefer the term big-boned," I said. "I have big bones. It's in my genes."

"Maybe I could go see a doctor?" Dooley asked. "I do feel a little weak."

"Sure," Odelia said, ignoring my groans of exasperation. "Why don't we go see Vena? That way you can relax. And we better take you, too, Max."

I gulped. "Me? Go see Vena? Why? I mean, why? Why Vena? Why?"

"Because when we went to see her last year she said you were too big for your size, and she wanted to put you on a diet, remember?"

I remembered. What a horrible suggestion! I'm not too big. It's my bones. "But I followed the diet," I reminded her. "I did everything she told me to."

"Yes, and she also said we should come back in a year so she could check."

"But… I don't want to go. I'm fine. I followed the diet. I—I'm good."

"We're going," she said firmly. "End of discussion."

I gave Dooley an angry look. "This is all your fault," I grumbled. "If you hadn't gone all hypochondriac on us this would never have happened."

"Max, be nice to Dooley. If he thinks there's something wrong with him, we better have him looked at. And you, mister, were never going to escape Vena."

"I wasn't?"

"Of course not. She has you scheduled for next month. But since we're taking Dooley anyway, she can take a look at you, too."

I just knew what she was going to say. She was going to say I hadn't lost enough weight and she was going to put me on that rotten diet again. Eating nothing but diet kibble for six months. No special treats. No chicken liver. No yummy surprises. "Just so you know, that diet stuff tastes like cardboard," I said.

"Well, you better hope that you lost enough weight, then," said Odelia.

No sympathy. No sympathy whatsoever. Humans are cruel. Just plain cruel.

"Oh, and we're taking Diego, too. He has to get his shots and he has to be neutered."

I shared a happy look with Dooley. Humans. Aren't they the best?

Odelia tapped her space bar and a video started playing on her screen.

"This is some raw footage from *Kitchen Disasters*. Niklaus used to upload snippets for his upcoming show to his website. Now watch this."

I watched this, and so did Dooley. All I saw was this Niklaus guy yelling and screaming at a chubby guy with a chef hat. The chef just kept on decorating a plate, looking thoroughly uncomfortable, his face a very unhealthy pasty white, until Niklaus snatched the plate out of his hands and dumped its contents into a trash can. The chef looked absolutely horrified after that, as if someone had taken his baby and thrown it away.

Odelia pressed the space bar again. "That was Hendrik Serarols being chewed out by Niklaus. Fun stuff, huh?"

"Pretty brutal," I said.

"Yeah, that Niklaus guy was not very nice," Dooley commented.

"No, he sure wasn't," Odelia said, swiveling in her office chair.

She picked up the phone. When it connected, she said, "Chase, any word on the Echo alibi?"

She pressed a button on her phone, and suddenly we could hear Chase's voice. "To get the information from Amazon would take weeks, and require a warrant—maybe even a court order. Luckily the Stowes were so kind to let me listen in on their account. Did you know you can play back your own audio recordings and delete them if you want?"

"No, I did not know that. So was it as bad as I think it was?"

"A lot of moaning and giggling. Turns out they asked Alexa to give them instructions."

"Instructions on what?"

He laughed. "What do you think, Poole? How to clean the sink? They asked Alexa to read them the entire *Kama Sutra*. They got to chapter five last night. And they ordered a bunch of saucy stuff on Amazon as well."

I could see that Odelia was blushing slightly, and I wondered what this Kama thing was. I nudged Dooley, but he was still looking depressed. No amount of giggling and moaning could cheer him up.

"So their alibi checked out, huh?"

"Pretty much. First time I had to listen in on a couple's recordings with the couple present. Brainard looked pretty proud of himself. Isabella? Not so much. She looked like she'd rather be anywhere but there. Still, it got them off the hook, so I'm guessing they're fine."

"So that's one suspect you can scratch from your list."

"Unfortunately, yes. What have you got so far?"

"I talked to Mrs. Niklaus Skad. Also known as Cybil Truscott."

And while Odelia regaled Chase with the story of her meeting with Mrs. Truscott, I jumped from the desk, and so did Dooley. Frankly I'd heard enough. The investigation was still nowhere, and what was even worse: I was going to have to face Vena Aleman again, my worst nightmare. Not that the veterinarian is a bad person. She's not. But she has this penchant for needles. It seems that each time Odelia takes me to see her she has to stick a needle in me. I hate it. They say it's for my own good, but I doubt it. I secretly suspect her of being a sadist. And a sadist with a medical degree is a very bad thing. Especially for us cats, who are pretty much defenseless.

"So are you happy with yourself now, Dooley?" I asked as we left the Happy Bays Gazette office and ambled down the street. "Now you've got us both going to Vena again. And you know what happens when we go to Vena. We get stuck with needles. Needles in the butt, needles in the neck, needles in the tummy. You name it, she sticks it."

"If only one of her needles will save my life," said Dooley.

I had to admit he did look like he was about to die. All because of the power of suggestion.

"You've got nothing to worry about. Since there's nothing

wrong with you Vena will just give you a clean bill of health and a hit with the needle. Me? She's going to put me on that scale again and decide I'm still too fat for my size and she's going to put me on a diet *and* stick me with the needle." I sighed. "What did I ever do to deserve this?"

At least Vena would neuter Diego. It was a small consolation.

"Do you think Vena can cure cancer?"

"If she could, she'd be a billionaire now."

"Oh."

"Yeah."

He gave me a sad look. "I want you to know I've always considered you my best friend, Max. And when I'm gone, could you look after Harriet for me?"

"You look after Harriet. You're going to outlive us all, buddy. It's the thin ones that live to be forty."

"Forty? There's no cat alive who's forty."

"There was this one cat who lived to be thirty-eight. She's in the Guinness Book of Records. I'm sure someone will best her and beat her record one day."

"Well, it won't be me," Dooley said gloomily. "I won't live another week."

I groaned. Was I really going to have to listen to this for much longer? "You're fine, Dooley. Even Odelia said you're fine."

"Odelia's no doctor."

"Her dad's a doctor."

"So?"

"So it's in her genes. That kind of stuff runs in the family."

He gave me a dubious look. "Being a doctor is a genetic thing?"

"Sure," I lied brazenly. "Didn't you ever watch *Diagnosis: Murder*? Dick Van Dyke's son was a doctor, too, remember? It's all in the genes!" He seemed to perk up, so I continued.

"So when Odelia tells you you're fine, you can rest assured she knows what she's talking about. She's got the, um, doctor gene."

"You're not saying that just to make me feel better?"

I was saying that to make *me* feel better. "Of course not! Everybody knows that's how it works. Trust me. Odelia knows."

He bobbed his head. "Thanks, Max. It's like a weight off my shoulders."

I clapped my paw on those same shoulders. "You're fine, buddy! The picture of health!"

"Phew. And here I was thinking I was a goner."

"Imagine that."

He shivered. "I've imagined that ever since we talked to Montserrat, so no thank you. I won't be imagining that anymore. I was actually feeling really sick."

"Power of the mind, Dooley. It's all up here." I tapped his noggin.

"What is up there, Max?"

In his case? Not much. "Your mind, Dooley. Whatever your mind pictures, your body carries out."

"So, if my mind pictured a nice juicy chicken wing, my body will somehow get it for me?"

"Sure," I said. "You just have to think hard enough and it'll happen."

"Wow, that's great, Max. Why don't I try that right now?" And he closed his eyes, presumably thinking very hard about chicken wings.

You're telling me that wasn't a very nice thing to do to my best friend? I think it was the best thing I could have done. At least he wasn't thinking about his imminent death anymore. Now he was thinking about the imminent death of a chicken. Hey, better a dead chicken than a dead Dooley, right?

CHAPTER 10

*W*hen Odelia ended the conversation with Chase she discovered that Max and Dooley had skedaddled. Which didn't surprise her. Max hated going to the vet, and Dooley seemed convinced he was about to die. She got up from her desk and found Dan leaning against the doorjamb.

"So? How's the investigation going?"

"So far the most likely suspect is the chef."

"Isn't it always?" he quipped with a twinkle in his eye.

"Chase seems to be convinced the couple running the restaurant didn't do it, and I talked to Skad's wife and she claims she has a solid alibi."

"Which you will undoubtedly go check."

"Undoubtedly," she said with a smile.

"So did I hear you talking to your cats again?" Dan asked.

"Dooley isn't feeling well," she said cautiously. Dan didn't know she could talk to her cats, though she suspected he had some idea of what was going on. They'd never discussed it, though, and she wasn't going to risk her career at the newspaper by admitting that her cats were the source of many of her best and most exclusive stories.

"I can imagine it must be quite a burden looking out for—how many cats do you have now?"

"Four—and it's not a burden. My mom and Gran take care of them, too, so it's no biggie."

"You know, when I hired you all those years ago, I partly did so because I figured you were young and you were going to go after the stories with the freshness and zeal that I'm lacking, due to my advanced age."

"You're not old, Dan," she protested.

"Wait," he said, holding up his hand. "Let me finish. But I also hired you on a hunch. Someone had told me once that the Poole women are special. That they have a feline streak. That they understand cats more than the rest of us do. My hunch proved correct. You're a better reporter than I ever was, and that's saying something, as I launched this damn paper."

She wondered what he was trying to say, if anything. "Thanks, Dan. That's high praise coming from you."

"You take good care of those cats for me, won't you? And tell them thanks."

She reddened. "I, um—I'm sure I don't know what you mean. Cats can't talk."

"No, but they can listen. And they ask the right questions." He tapped his nose. "And that, my dear, are the hallmarks of a great reporter."

She left the office wondering if she shouldn't have protested more. Now it looked like she was accepting Dan's idea that somehow she could talk to her cats. Then again, she hadn't admitted anything, and if she knew Dan, she was sure he'd keep her secret.

She arrived at the police station and saw that Chase's car was gone. She walked into the squat one-story building and breezed past Dolores, who manned the front desk. She gave her a wave and walked right through to her uncle's office at the end of the hallway. She knocked and stepped inside without waiting for a reply.

Her uncle was sitting with his feet up on his desk when she entered, and she took a seat across from him, also putting her feet up. "So Max and Dooley talked to Erin Coka's cat Montserrat, who told them another cat, this one called Fred, not that it matters, saw a black Tesla parked in the alley behind the restaurant last night. Just thought you'd like to know."

Her uncle took pad and pencil and wrote down, "Anonymous witness sees black Tesla parked in alley behind *Fry Me for an Oyster*." He looked up. "Plates?"

"No plates."

He smiled. "That would have been too easy. Anything else your feline detectives discovered?"

"I found out something." She told him about her conversation with Cybil Truscott and her uncle whistled.

"Now there's a nice, juicy suspect if I ever saw one. Motive, opportunity... I think she might even have managed to get the body up in the oven. Big, strong woman, right?"

"Not big, but I'll bet pure rage would have fueled her. She's the vindictive type."

"Real ball-buster, huh?" He picked up his pad again, and wrote, tongue between his teeth, "Talk to pool boy at Hampton Springs Hotel."

"Any word from the coroner?"

"Just got a call from him, as a matter of fact. Found a fortune cookie in the victim's stomach."

"A fortune cookie? What did it say?"

"Someone special will soon enter your life."

"Huh. Guess that must have referred to the killer."

"He or she certainly left an indelible impression."

They shared a smile. Gallows humor was typical for cops and reporters alike. "What else did he find? Cause of death?" she asked.

Uncle Alec shook his head and shifted his bulk in his chair, which creaked under his weight. "Abe says it's hard to figure out what happened when the integrity of the body has been compromised to such an extent. He's still trying to find out, but so far he couldn't determine cause of death."

"Maybe toxicology will tell us something."

"It certainly wasn't a bullet that killed him, or a blow to the head. That would have been obvious. Strangulation? Impossible to determine. Knife wound? So far nothing indicates he was stabbed."

"What happens if Abe isn't able to discover a cause of death?"

"It'll just make things a little harder for us. We won't have a murder weapon to look for, or an MO to use to pinpoint the killer."

She nodded. "So Chase told me about the Echo?"

Her uncle laughed. "Yeah, that was something. And good thing they decided to come clean. Getting Amazon to release the recordings would have been tricky."

"I think it's smart they came forward. They must have known they'd be the prime suspects until their alibi was confirmed."

"Maybe you and Chase could get one of these Echo contraptions. Spice up your love life."

She gave him a dark look. "Chase and I have no love life to spice up. We're not dating, Uncle Alec."

"Then maybe you should start. I think you guys would be great together. I know for a fact he likes you, Odelia. Likes you a lot."

"He... he told you?"

"He didn't have to. I can tell from the way he talks about

69

you. He admires the hell out of you. Thinks you'd make a great detective."

"That's because he doesn't know… my little secret."

"He doesn't have to know. Besides, even without Max and Dooley you still make a great detective. You just have a knack for it."

"Thanks. It's just that… what if he found out? I mean, not just for me. I have to think about Mom and Gran, too. Nobody can find out. They'd just label us freaks. And the attention that would garner would destroy us."

"Nobody is going to find out, honey," he said softly. "And even if Chase got an inkling, I'm sure he wouldn't mind. And he definitely wouldn't tell on you."

"I don't know," she said. "It's much harder to keep something like that a secret when you're involved with a person."

"Of course. And if you are serious about him, I think sooner or later you're going to have to come clean."

She shook her head. "Never. I'd rather not date him than tell him."

"Then you'd be making a big mistake," he warned her.

"It would be an even bigger mistake to tell him," she insisted. "He wouldn't understand. Nobody does."

"I do."

"That's different, Uncle Alec. You're family. You grew up with it. Chase is—"

"Chase could be family. I know the boy, Odelia. He's got a good heart."

She was still shaking her head when the Chief's phone rang. He picked up with a jovial, "Lay it on me!" He listened for a moment, then his face fell and he removed his feet from the desk. "Well, I'll be damned. Are you sure it's her? Uh-huh. Okay. I'll be right over." He hung up and stared at Odelia.

"Well? What is it?" she insisted.

"It's your grandmother. There's been an incident."

Her heart constricted as she shot up from her chair. "Is she all right?"

The Chief grinned. "More than all right, apparently. There's talk of indecent exposure."

She closed her eyes. "Oh, no."

"Oh, yes. Several beachgoers complained to one of the lifeguards near Pyke Point that an old woman and an old guy were going at it on the beach, in full view of the other visitors. The lifeguard called the cops and your gran and the guy have both been placed under arrest." He shook his head. "I never thought that the day would come I'd have to bust my own mother for lurid behavior."

"If it's any consolation, I never thought the day would come I'd be embarrassed by my own grandmother."

"Well," said Uncle Alec, getting up and slipping on his gun belt. "The day has come, honey. So let's see what she's got to say for herself, shall we?"

$\mathcal{D}$ooley and I were strutting our stuff along the beach. Dooley had been trying hard to picture a nice fat juicy chicken wing but so far he wasn't having any luck.

"It's not working, Max," he lamented.

"Just keep on trying. You have to give it some time."

"But I'm trying very hard."

"Creating stuff with your mind is just like with all other stuff, Dooley," I told him sternly. "It takes a lot of practice."

"Do you think so?"

"Sure! Do you think Beyoncé popped out of the womb and sang like a nightingale? Of course not! Or do you think Garfield could eat all of that lasagna straight out of the gate? The cat had to train his stomach! Took years!"

"Yes, I see," he said, nodding seriously. "So if I keep on trying it'll happen, right?"

"It will happen, Dooley," I assured him. "You just keep on visualizing chicken wings and they will come flying. At first maybe you'll just get a few feathers, then maybe a bone, but eventually the chicken wings will come your way and you'll be able to feast on them to your heart's content."

"All right," he finally said, fully convinced now. "Like you said, it all takes practice. So I'll just practice very hard from now on. Practice practice practice. I'll be thinking about chicken wings morning, noon and night and they will come."

"That's the spirit," I said, glad he'd finally stopped moaning about his imminent death. So what if chicken wings would dominate our conversations from now on? It was way better than talk about dying, right?

We hopped up on a bench some smart town planners had placed along the boardwalk and gazed out across the ocean. That's the beauty of a town like Hampton Cove. When being cooped inside your home gets too much for you, you take a stroll along the beach and sniff up some of that refreshing ocean breeze. You have to ignore the thousands of tourists that occupy the beach, of course, sizzling in the sun. It's a custom I've never gotten my head around. Who wants to voluntarily go lie on the sand to be baked alive? I just don't get it. Good thing us cats are way smarter than that. You'll never find us slathering ourselves in oil to be broiled or sautéed.

Humans. They're nuts. But what are you gonna do?

And we sat there watching men building castles out of sand, women jumping over waves, kids filling buckets and then pouring them out again and other humans engaging in other equally pointless activities when suddenly there was some kind of altercation not far from where we sat.

"Hey," Dooley said, giving me a nudge. "Isn't that Grandma Poole?"

Grandma Poole's name isn't actually Poole but Muffin. Vesta Muffin. But for convenience's sake everyone calls her Grandma Poole. Sounds a lot better than Grandma Muffin. I glanced over to where Dooley was pointing. An elderly woman and an elderly man were lying on a beach towel, hugging and kissing. And from what I could see, there was some nekkid involved.

"Are you sure? I don't think Gran would ever—oh, heck, you're right. It's Gran, all right."

"Of course it's Gran. Do you really think I wouldn't recognize my own human? But what is she doing, Max?"

"Um…" Now this was going to be awkward. "Remember when *Basic Instinct* was on television the other night? And Odelia switched it off because there were parts that she felt uncomfortable to let us watch?"

"Oh, yes. That was way weird, huh? Some woman in some bed with some man and then suddenly there was a knife and then the woman had no clothes on?"

"Yes, that was way weird. Well, the same thing is happening with Grandma Poole right now. So I think we better not watch, Dooley."

"You think watching it will be bad for us, Max?"

"It might be bad for our sense of taste," I said.

We weren't the only ones who'd noticed the frolicking old folks. Some parents close to the couple were averting their children's eyes, while one guy was brazenly filming everything with his smartphone. Then a few irate parents approached the nearest lifeguard, who got on the phone.

"Uh-oh," I said. "Looks like Gran's in trouble."

"You mean Odelia will be cross with her?"

"I think everyone will be cross with her." Not that she'd mind. Gran doesn't care. She does whatever she wants and listens to no one. She's a free spirit who gets more and more out of control with each passing year. At least that's what Odelia's mom Marge always says. I don't know if it's true. Seems to me that when you're as old as Gran, most people give you a free pass. But not today. As we watched, a police vehicle trundled up.

"Are the police going to arrest Gran?" Dooley asked.

"Looks like it. Though I'm sure that once they realize she's the Chief's mother, they might reconsider."

"Why is that?"

"Because if they're like most people, they like to hang on to their jobs."

"You mean Uncle Alec will fire them if they arrest Gran?"

"Maybe not fire them outright, but he'll definitely reprimand them."

"What's reprimand?"

"What you get when what you do isn't what others think you should do."

"You mean like when Brutus and Harriet got together and I didn't like it?"

"Exactly like that."

"I should have reprimanded Brutus."

"He would have beaten you."

"I can never win, can I?"

"Nope. That's why we snitch on Brutus so Odelia can reprimand him."

We watched as the officers approached Gran and her gentleman friend. Gran was talking very loudly, as if offended that anyone would be offended. Her friend just sat there, looking like the Sphinx of Giza. Yes, I watch *National Geographic*. And the *Discovery Channel*.

"Looks like they're reprimanding Gran," Dooley said. "And she's reprimanding them."

"And here's Chief Alec to reprimand them all," I said.

The Chief and Odelia had driven up in the Chief's squad car and parked just next to our bench. He quickly descended the few steps to the beach and trudged through the powdery sand, looking none too happy.

Odelia joined us on the bench.

"So what happened?" she asked.

"Well, it was just like in *Basic Instinct*," Dooley said. "But without the knife. And when Max told me to look away, I did," he quickly added.

Odelia laughed. "Good for you. Watching that could have scarred you for life."

Dooley's eyes went wide. "You think so?"

"Didn't I tell you? She's a doctor," I said. "She knows."

Dooley gulped. "Good thing I looked away when I did. My health isn't what it used to be and I don't think I should take any chances right now."

"I'm not a doctor, Max," Odelia said.

"No, but your dad is, and that kind of thing runs in the family," I said, desperately winking at her in the hope she would catch my drift.

She arched an eyebrow. "Oh, I see what you mean. Because I said Dooley is in perfect health, right?"

"Right!" I said, nodding.

"What's wrong with your eye, Max?" Dooley asked worriedly.

"Oh, just a twitch," I said. "I get it from time to time."

"You shouldn't have watched Gran and that old man," he scolded me. "Now see what you've done. Your eye will never be the same."

Odelia leaned in and took a look at my eye. "Mh," she said with a faux-serious look on her face. "I think I'll be able to save it, Max."

Dooley sighed with admiration. "I'm so glad you're a doctor, Odelia. What would Max do without you? Or me, for that matter? I thought I was dying, and you saved me. And you, of course, Max. You're the best friend."

"Thanks, Dooley. I love you, too," I said.

"And thanks to Max I'm going to get all the chicken I want," Dooley continued.

"Oh? Is that a fact?" Odelia asked, her lips twitching into a smile.

"Max explained to me how the power of the mind can accomplish anything. So I've been thinking about chicken wings nonstop, and soon they're going to start materializing. I'll have more chicken wings than I'll know what to do with!"

"Just be careful you don't start thinking about Gran and that old man," Odelia teased. "Or else that's what you'll get instead of chicken."

Dooley's lips formed in a perfect O. "Oh. My. God! And now Gran and that old man *are* all I can think of! What is this witchcraft?!"

"Just relax, Dooley," Odelia said. "I was just teasing you. Your mind may be strong, but it's not that strong. But I think you'll find that if you just ask Gran for a piece of chicken, she'll be happy to give it to you."

"Unless she's in jail," I said, gesturing at Chief Alec going toe to toe with his mother.

"She's not going to jail," Odelia assured us. "She's just going to get a slap on the wrist."

"And a reprimand," Dooley added.

Odelia laughed. "I see you've been adding new words to your vocabulary. Well done, Dooley."

"Max taught me. He's been teaching me a lot."

Odelia cut a critical eye at me. "So I see. Maybe too much, huh, Max?"

I shrugged. "Just trying to help."

"Yeah, right," she said with a smirk.

Gran got dressed, and so did the elderly gentleman she was having relations with. All around, people were watching, and the man with the smartphone was still filming. This whole thing would probably be on the Internet tonight.

"Show's over, folks!" the Chief was shouting, holding up

his hands. "Go back to your business. And you, you better stop filming, buddy," he told the man.

An older couple had posted themselves next to us. They were shaking their heads in disapproval. "The exact same thing happened last night at the hotel," the woman told Odelia apropos of nothing.

"These two were at the hotel?" Odelia asked.

"No, not these two. Another couple. We're staying at the Hampton Springs Hotel," the woman explained. "And down by the pool Cybil Truscott was behaving very inappropriately with the pool boy." She pursed her lips disapprovingly. "They were… fornicating. On the pool beds! Right under our noses! I couldn't sleep so I caught the whole thing. An absolute disgrace!"

"We complained to management, of course," said her husband.

"Not that they'll do anything," the woman added. "Because Cybil Truscott is a star, and we're just lowly guests of the hotel. So she can get away with murder."

Odelia looked up, and both Dooley and I pricked up our ears. "Murder?" Odelia asked.

"Just a figure of speech," said the woman. "Though I'm sure she could get away with murder. Did you hear about her husband that got killed last night?"

"But if she was… fornicating right under your noses, surely she couldn't have done it," Odelia said.

The woman frowned. This hadn't occurred to her. "Well, no, but she could have hired a person to do it for her."

"Like a hitman," said her husband. "Those rich folks do it all the time. Don't like your husband? Pay someone to kill him. It's a common thing in Hollywood."

I didn't know about that, and neither did Odelia, apparently, for she wrinkled her nose dubiously. "Did you tell the police about the pool boy thing?"

"Oh, no!" said the woman. "Far be it from us to get involved with the police."

"I'm sure the police know all about it," her husband clarified. "I mean, the entire hotel saw the lurid scene! They were all on their balconies, shaking their heads in absolute dismay."

"But that didn't keep them from watching," Odelia muttered.

Grandma came trudging up to us, and the tourists stalked off, their faces contorted into expressions of condemnation.

"Alec says he'll give me a ride home," Gran said. "Not that I want a ride home, mind you. I was having so much fun with Leo, until some people started complaining." She gave a disgusted grunt. "I just wish they'd all mind their own business for a change. I mean, what's wrong with having a little fun at the beach?"

"There's nothing wrong with having a little fun as long as you don't do it in front of a bunch of families with kids, Gran," Odelia said. "So please don't do it again, all right?"

"Now that's a reprimand," I whispered to Dooley.

"That's what I figured," he whispered back. He stole a glance at Gran. "So do you think it's too soon for me to ask for that piece of chicken?"

CHAPTER 12

*C*hief Alec drove Odelia and Gran to the Hampton Springs Hotel. Odelia wanted to check the story of Cybil Truscott and the pool boy so they could scratch the widow off their list of suspects. They entered the hotel and the Chief asked the clerk at the reception desk about the incident of last night. The clerk immediately blushed.

"Um, yes, that happened," the young man said. He had red hair and freckles and a hard time suppressing a grin.

"So where can we find the male star of this auspicious event?" the Chief asked.

The guy gestured at the pool area. "Dale's working today, though from the looks of things he won't be for much longer."

"Why is that?" Odelia asked.

"Hotel rules. We're not supposed to get too friendly with the guests."

"And Dale broke that rule," the Chief said, nodding.

"He got *way* too friendly," he said, that grin finally breaking through. "Way and way too friendly from what I heard."

"Right," said the Chief, tapping the desk. "Thanks, buddy."

They walked outside, and Gran said, "I don't get it. This Truscott woman can make a spectacle of herself in front of the entire hotel and I can't even spend some time at the beach with my lover? That's just not right, Alec!"

"There's a difference between what people do in the privacy of their pool in the middle of the night and what they do on a public beach during the day," he grumbled.

"But this isn't Truscott's private pool. This is the hotel pool."

"Nobody complained," the Chief said. "No complaint, no problem."

"I should have ducked behind the bushes," Gran grumbled. "But Leo doesn't like the bushes. Says it feels too sneaky. And he doesn't like sneaky."

"Sounds like Leo is quite a pistol," said Uncle Alec.

"Sounds like Leo is a bad influence," Odelia said.

She shared a look with her uncle. "Or the other way around," the latter muttered. She smiled. He just might be right. Leo didn't really look like the kind of guy who'd go out of his way to cause trouble. In fact he looked one cardiac arrest away from a trip to the morgue. If anyone was the pistol here, it was Gran.

They stepped onto the paved pool area and searched around for the infamous pool boy. There were plenty of hotel guests lounging on pool beds and chaise lounges, sipping cocktails and reading the latest summer bestseller. Then she spotted a young man messing around with what looked like a filter near the edge of the pool. He was tan with brown hair, dressed in blue dolphin boxers and looked way too young to be entertaining Mrs. Truscott in the middle of the night.

They headed over while Gran made herself comfortable on one of the chaise lounges. Chief Alec had sworn not to let his mother out of his sight for the rest of the day, or anywhere near Leo. His officers had wanted to put her under arrest, but when they discovered who she was, had balked at the prospect of arresting their boss's mother. To save face, Alec had told them he'd personally guarantee something like this didn't happen again. At least not today.

"Hey there, son," the Chief said as they approached the kid.

He looked up, shielding his eyes from the sun. "Yes?"

"Alec Lip. Chief of Police. Can I have a word with you?"

The kid rose to his feet. He looked like he'd been expecting this. "Yes?" His eyes darted to Odelia, a question mark forming on his face.

"Oh, this is Odelia Poole. My niece. She's helping me investigate the murder of Niklaus Skad. So it's Dale, right? Dale…."

The kid licked his lips. He didn't look a day over twenty. "Dale Hoover, sir."

"Well, Dale Hoover, we're trying to ascertain the whereabouts of Niklaus Skad's wife last night. I believe you're familiar with Cybil Truscott?"

"I… I don't believe I am, sir. Is she a guest at the hotel?"

"Oh, yes, she is. And we heard you *are* familiar with Mrs. Truscott." He gave Dale a knowing look. "Very familiar, if you know what I mean."

"I—I'm sure I don't know, sir," Dale stammered, blushing beneath his tan.

"You and Cybil were seen going at it last night in the pool," Odelia explained.

"At it? I don't know…"

"Come on, son. I don't have to draw you a picture, do I?" the Chief asked.

"The entire hotel saw you, Dale," Odelia said. She gestured up, and Dale followed her gesture. His face fell. The entire hotel was built around the pool area, five floors of balconied rooms all looking out across the pool.

"Oh…" he said, now looking positively mortified. "Oh, well damn."

"Yes, that's the expression I would have used," said the Chief with a sympathetic smile. "I take it you didn't know you had witnesses?"

"No, I did not, sir," said the kid, gulping slightly.

"One thing you should know about women like Cybil Truscott, son," said the Chief. "They love attention. In fact they crave it. So while you may not have been aware that this spot is a very public one, even at night, she certainly did."

"I was expecting her to invite me up to her room, but she insisted we stay here. She said the water…" He gulped again. "The water acted like an aphrodisiac."

"Right," Odelia said skeptically. More like the attention.

"Do you have a girlfriend, Dale?" asked the Chief.

He nodded. "High school sweetheart, sir. If she finds out about this…"

"I'll bet she won't be too well pleased."

"Please don't tell her about it," he pleaded.

"I'm not going to tell her anything, but stuff like this is bound to come out sooner or later. Especially since a bunch of those folks up there on those balconies had phones, and it's more than likely a few of them filmed the whole thing."

"Oh, crap," he said, raking his hands through his hair. "Oh, God."

"You better tell her yourself," Odelia said. "Before she hears it from a 'friend.' Or, worse, gets a link to the video."

He nodded, now looking a little pale around the nostrils. "I will, Miss Poole. I will tell her the moment my shift ends."

"And next time you want to get involved with a hotel guest, think twice, Dale," the Chief admonished him.

"Yes, sir," said Dale.

They left the kid looking absolutely crestfallen. "It's not going to happen again," Odelia told her uncle. "Because he won't be working here for much longer."

"He won't be working here for much longer, but he'll work at some other hotel, and the same thing will happen again. He's a handsome looking kid, and women like Cybil Truscott prey on young men like him, just for their own personal satisfaction." He shook his head. "At least now we know she didn't kill her husband."

"Unless she hired a hitman."

He laughed. "Is that your latest theory?"

"Just something I heard from some tourists. Turns out all Hollywood stars hire hitmen to kill their spouses these days. It's the latest craze."

"Gee, I didn't know that. Pretty bloody custom, if you ask me."

They reached the chaise lounge Gran had selected for her own. She was sleeping soundly, her head back and her mouth open, snoring softly.

"Maybe we should let her sleep?" Odelia suggested. "She's had a rough day."

"She had a rough day? I had a rough day. She can sleep at home," he said. He reached down and shook her shoulder. "Wake up, Mom. Time to go home."

She opened her eyes and licked her lips. "I just had the most wonderful dream. Leo was suddenly fifty years younger but he still wanted me." Then her eyes fell on Dale Hoover. "Oh, my. Looks like my dream just came true."

"Not happening, Mom," said Uncle Alec. "The kid is already spoken for."

"And in enough trouble with his girlfriend as it is," Odelia added.

"Dang," Gran said, getting up with a groan. "Why is it that

the good ones always are? I could have used a young 'un for a change."

"Let's get you out of here before you cause a fuss," said Alec.

"I don't cause a fuss," she said. "I never cause a fuss. It's the others that cause all the fuss. Damn bunch of busybodies. There should be a law against people messing with other's business." She gave her son a keen look. "You're a cop, Alec. Can't you make a law against nosy parkers?"

"I wish I could," he said with a grin. "But if I did you'd be the first to be thrown in jail, and we can't have that now, can we?"

"You'd throw your own mother in jail?"

"The law is the law. Can't bend it just for you, Mom."

"Oh, hell. What good is it to have a cop for a son if he can't even keep you out of jail?"

"I kept you out of jail now, didn't I? Indecent exposure is a serious offense, Mom."

"Poppycock. It's the beach. Everybody's indecently exposed. It's ageism is what it is. Pure ageism. There should be a law against ageism."

And so it went on, until they arrived at the library. Odelia was glad to drop Gran off with her mom. She loved her to pieces, but a little of the old woman went a long way, and for now she'd had more than her fill.

CHAPTER 13

*W*e got home fully expecting to find Brutus and Harriet in the throes of a touching make-up scene. Instead, the moment we walked in, we were shocked once again. Just like on the beach, Dooley and I were forced to close our eyes when we caught Diego and Harriet on the couch—my couch!—doing the kind of stuff Odelia had warned Gran about.

"Omigod!" Dooley cried, immediately averting his eyes. "It burns! It burns, Max!"

Unlike Dooley, I had the opposite reaction. I couldn't stop staring. It was like a train wreck. I just couldn't look away. All I saw was a lot of orange, a lot of white, and a lot of pink. In my own home! On my own couch!

This was just too much. This was just... And then I heard it. A soft sobbing sound. It seemed to come from somewhere nearby. I glanced at Dooley, thinking it was him, but he was still squeezing his eyes tightly shut. The sobbing seemed to come from somewhere close by, though. So I went in search of it, and then I saw a shadow flit by. It was a dark shadow, and it hurtled past us with such speed that it was like a black blur. The shadow streaked out the window and was gone.

Harriet and Diego didn't seem to mind that they'd suddenly gained an audience. They just kept smooching and making weird kissing sounds. Yuck.

So I walked out, gesturing for Dooley to come along. But since he still had his eyes closed, that didn't work.

"Dooley," I hissed. "Let's get out of here!"

"I'm not opening my eyes, Max," he promised me. "No way am I opening them. If I do I might not survive. And since my health isn't what it used to be, I'm not taking any chances!"

"Oh, all right," I grumbled, and guided him to the French windows and out.

The fresh air did me a world of good. "You can open your eyes now," I said. "We're safe."

He first opened one eye, then the other one, and looked relieved. "Phew, that was a close call, huh?"

"Yeah. Did you see that shadow? No, of course you didn't."

"I did hear the sobbing," he said. "Do you think that was Brutus?"

I eyed him intently. "You think so?"

He nodded. "Imagine walking in on your girlfriend with… that."

I shivered. "Yeah, I see what you mean."

We both looked at the house next door, where Dooley lived with Brutus and Harriet. The hedge between the two gardens had a large hole in it, and we slipped through it, preparing ourselves for the worst. Then I halted. "Are you sure we should get involved? I mean, Brutus isn't exactly our buddy."

"I think everybody needs a friend in their hour of need,

Max," Dooley said earnestly. "Even though Brutus isn't everyone's cup of tea, he's a cat in need."

"Oh, all right," I said on a sigh, and we padded into the next backyard. And there he was. The big, bad brute. Sitting on the back porch swing and crying his heart out. Even though I'd never gotten along with the cat, my heart went out to him.

We hopped up on the swing and glanced at one another. I'm not exactly the world's best Samaritan. I mean, if I applied to work at the crisis counseling hotline they probably wouldn't accept me.

I cleared my throat awkwardly. "There, there," I murmured, raising my paw to clap Brutus on the shoulder. "There's a lot of other cats out there."

In response, he just sobbed louder, his shoulder shaking. "Go away!"

"Max!" Dooley hissed. "Not helping!"

"I don't see you trying!" I hissed back.

"I went through this, you know," Dooley told Brutus.

"Just… go away!" Brutus sniffed, turning away from us. It was obvious he was embarrassed that we would see him like this.

"It's actually a funny story," said Dooley, undeterred. "You came into our lives and got involved with Harriet and I was the one feeling sad."

"It's karma," I said.

"Max!" Dooley loud-whispered, giving me a look of abhorrence.

"Well, it is, isn't it?" I asked. Crisis counseling? Not my strong suit.

"It will pass, you know," said Dooley, addressing Brutus once again.

"It will?" asked Brutus in a strangled voice.

"It will," Dooley assured him. "I'm over Harriet now. Seeing her with another cat does nothing to me."

I gave him a critical look.

"Oh, all right. It does something. But I don't fall to pieces over it anymore."

"I'm not falling to pieces," Brutus said, his voice smothered. "I just got something in my eye."

"Of course you have," I said. "A big chunk of Diego, right?"

Brutus produced the loudest wail yet, and Dooley was back to rolling his eyes at me. I shrugged and mouthed, 'What?'

'Shut. Up!' he mouthed back.

"Did you see her?" Brutus asked now.

"Yeah, we saw her," Dooley said with his best pastor's voice.

"Was she still… you know?"

"Yep, she was still giving mouth-to-mouth to that orange menace," I said.

"Oh, God!" Brutus cried, and buried his head in his paws. "Why?!"

"It's just a fling," Dooley said. "She'll snap out of it. She's just temporarily blinded by passion. Once the initial zing wears off, she'll see Diego for what he really is: a cad and a nasty piece of work. Trust me, Brutus, once she sees through him she'll come crawling back to you."

Now it was my turn to make eyes at Dooley. I pointed at him. "Come back to you, you mean," I whispered.

He shook his head. "I'm in the friend zone, Max. I've always been in the friend zone, and I'll always stay there as far as Harriet is concerned. And I'm fine with that. There are more important things in life than being Harriet's boyfriend."

"No, there are not!" Brutus wailed.

I went back to patting the big guy on the back. "There, there," I muttered, for lack of anything better to say.

"I promise you, Brutus," Dooley said, making a last-ditch attempt to get Brutus to back away from the precipice. "This pain will go away."

For the first time, he looked up. He looked horrible. His eyes were all red and weepy and his nose was all runny. He wasn't the Brutus I'd come to know and hate. Not by a long shot. "Promise?"

"Promise," Dooley said.

He gave us both a watery smile. "You guys are the best friends."

"That's what we're here for," I said blithely. Even though I'd shaken paws with Brutus and declared ourselves buds, I still had my doubts about his intentions. But now wasn't the time to get into all of that.

"Us cats have to stick together," Dooley said. "Hey! I've got an idea! Why don't I wrangle us up some chicken wings?"

"Can you do that?" Brutus asked between two sniffs.

Dooley tapped his brow with a knowing smile. "Power of the mind, Brutus. Power of the mind." And then he squinched his eyes shut and thought really hard, even placing his paws on his temples to speed up the process.

CHAPTER 14

That night, the whole family met for dinner. Tex had gotten his famous barbecue skills out and was overseeing the proceedings with his customary flair. Mom had baked a ginormous apple pie that now stood chilling on the kitchen windowsill. Gran had wanted to invite Leo over for dinner but Mom and Dad had put their foot down. No repetition of the beach scene in their house.

Chase had arrived, as Uncle Alec's guest, and had brought a bottle of the best—Chardonnay from the looks of it—and Odelia was happy to see him, which was a big change from before, when she used to scold her mom for inviting the burly cop. The cats were all there, except for Harriet and Diego, who were conspicuously absent. Brutus, Dooley and Max sat on the porch swing, looking on as dinner progressed, with Brutus looking like a shadow of his former self.

Odelia had no idea what was going on with him until she remembered about Diego making a pass at Harriet. Apparently the Persian's allegiances had shifted once again, and this time it was Brutus whose heart had been stomped on.

91

"So what's all this about a big murder investigation?" Dad asked as he placed a nice, fat kabob on her plate.

She added roasted baby potatoes with rosemary and garlic and dug in. "Famous chef got killed, Dad," she said. "Niklaus Skad."

"Oh, the *Kitchen Disasters* guy? I loved that show!"

Tex Poole, a bluff man with a shock of white hair, loved all cooking shows. He considered himself something of a *cuisinier*, though the only thing he did well was barbecue. Still, if it made him happy, that was all that mattered.

"Poor man," said Mom, a delicate, fair-haired woman. "I thought he was a little too harsh on his candidates from time to time, but I think he meant well."

"He was brutal," Uncle Alec said, dumping a glob of mayonnaise on his potatoes. "It was car crash television at its best."

"It wasn't that bad," said Gran, who'd been moping all this time. She was probably missing her Leo. "A lot of these so-called chefs can't cook for crap, and Niklaus Skad didn't mince words when he told them so. The fact that they couldn't cope was their problem, not his."

"I thought he was overly harsh," said Chase, munching down on a sausage. "The way he treated restaurateurs was uncalled for and more about boosting his ratings than a genuine desire to see those restaurants he selected do better."

She smiled at Chase. "That's exactly what I thought, but you put it so much better."

"I guess I have a way with words," said Chase.

"You've got a way with your lips," said Gran. "There's a difference."

"Mom," said Chief Alec warningly. "Let's keep it civilized."

"I am keeping it civilized. I'm just like Niklaus Skad: I say it like it is."

"Well, there's a difference between saying it like it is and intentionally hurting people, and Skad crossed that line many times on his show," said Alec.

"Which is probably what got him killed," Odelia added.

"Amen to that," her uncle said, clinking his glass of Chardonnay against hers.

"So how was the interview with Hendrik Serarols?" she asked. She'd forgotten to ask her uncle about that.

"He's a suspect," said her uncle.

"A very strong suspect," Chase added.

"Who's Hendrik Serarols?" asked Tex, flinging more kabobs on the grill.

"The chef at *Fry Me for an Oyster*," Odelia explained.

"He was the one who suffered the most abuse," Chase said. "There's a video online of Niklaus having a go at him." He shook his head. "Not pretty."

"I saw that," said Odelia. "So did he have an alibi for last night?"

"He does, but he doesn't want to supply it," said her uncle.

She frowned. "He's refusing to tell you where he was?"

"Yup. He says he was nowhere near the restaurant, but when I asked him where he was, he refused to tell me."

"That's odd," said Mom.

"That's suspicious," Gran said. "If you ask me, he did it."

"Let's not jump to conclusions," said Alec.

Chase dabbed at his lips with his napkin. "He had motive —he had opportunity—and he's certainly strong enough to have pulled this off. I say we have plenty of grounds for an arrest, Chief."

"And I say my gut tells me he didn't do it." They all looked down at Chief Alec's sizable gut, and he laughed. "Now don't start with me, you people." He patted his round belly. "A good chief needs bulk."

"A good chief needs muscle," Chase chided him.

"Fair enough. I have gained a few pounds. And I blame

my sister's cooking." He glanced at Marge, who smiled indulgently.

"A good chief needs to be fed properly," she said. "And I know that if I don't do it, you certainly won't."

That was true enough. After his wife had died, Uncle Alec had let himself go for a while, snacking on fast food and anything he could get his hands on. Since then, Mom had taken him under her wing, and now he ate out here most nights.

"Great food as usual, Mrs. Poole," said Chase appreciatively. "Doc."

"Thanks, Chase. It's nice to cook for someone who appreciates it," said Mom.

"I think you should lock up this chef and force him to supply you with an alibi," said Gran, who was starting to sound as harsh as Niklaus Skad.

Chief Alec grimaced. "I'm doing no such thing, Mother. And may I remind you that I'm the one in charge of this investigation and not you?"

"You reminding me won't stop me from giving you my opinion."

"So what happened to Leo?" Chase asked, giving Odelia a wink.

Gran shrugged. "How should I know? They've forbidden him from the house—kicked him out on his ear. The poor man is probably lying in a gutter somewhere, wondering what he did wrong." She wagged an admonishing finger. "You can't stop true love. You can beat us—you can arrest us —you can send us to the electric chair for all I care, but nothing will keep Leo and me apart. We're like Romeo and Juliet. Though Leo told me he's not going to try and climb to my balcony on account of his arthritis. That and he just had a hip replacement."

"Leo Wetland is married, Mom," Chief Alec said with a sigh.

"His wife is in a retirement home so that doesn't count," Gran said stubbornly. "She's no good to him all drugged up and bedridden and all."

"I just don't think it's very nice of him to run around with you while his wife is laid up is all," said Uncle Alec, throwing down his napkin.

"The man has needs," Gran insisted. "And so do I."

"So find yourself a decent man," Mom insisted. "Not this... weasel."

Gran narrowed her eyes into slits. "Who are you calling a weasel?"

"Leo! He should be by his wife's side—her aid and support."

"You know how hard it is for a girl to find a decent guy at my age?" Gran asked, changing tack. "There's so few good men out there."

"So? That doesn't mean you have to steal other people's husbands."

Gran threw up her hands. "If you're all going to gang up on me I've got nothing more to say. I'm out of here." At this, she got up, her chin in the air. Then she caught sight of Mom's apple pie and promptly sat down again. "Maybe after dessert."

"Don't you have any other suspects apart from this chef?" Dad asked.

The Chief leaned back, his hands on his belly. "Well, there's Skad's assistant. Stacie Roebuck. I haven't had a chance to talk to her yet, but she told one of my officers that she was in her hotel room all night. I don't think it'll be hard to verify that she was. Those rooms all have key cards, and the data is accessible to hotel security, complete with date and time stamp, so..."

"I heard she was pretty bullied by Niklaus," said Chase.

"Yes, she was," the Chief confirmed. "First line of fire and all that."

"She could have done it out of revenge," said Dad.

"Let's talk to her first thing tomorrow," said Uncle Alec. "In the meantime..." He eyed that apple pie longingly. "What's for dessert, Marge?"

Mom smiled. "Maybe you should skip dessert for once?"

There was a howl of protest, and it was obvious Uncle Alec wasn't about to go on a diet anytime soon.

"Wait," said Dad, getting up. "Before you bring out the pie, there's something I wanted to get off my chest."

They all looked at Dad, who was holding up his glass of wine. "Being here with you all warms my heart. And you know I appreciate you for joining my beautiful wife and me around the dinner table each and every night. But this isn't like any other night. In fact this is a very special night."

His eyes flickered with delight as Mom clapped a hand to her mouth. "Oh, Tex. You didn't..."

"I sure did. Today, thirty years ago, I met the most wonderful woman in the world."

"Who was she?" Alec quipped.

"She's sitting right here," said Tex. "It took me another five years to wear down her resistance and get her to say yes to me."

"We were too young, Tex," Mom said.

"You're still too young," Gran grumbled.

"And when finally she agreed to be my wife, she made me the happiest man in the world." He held up his glass in a salute. "Here's to you, Marge. I love you."

"I love you, Tex," Mom said, and then they all raised their glasses, and drank to the couple.

To Odelia's surprise, Dad got out a bulky package next, and placed it next to Mom's plate. "Just a small token of my appreciation for all that you do for our family on a daily basis," he said, taking a seat again.

"Oh, Tex," she said, a little flustered. "You shouldn't have."

Odelia saw that the packaging indicated the store was Ziv Riding's. So when Mom parted the paper and picked out a blouse, she wasn't surprised.

"Hey, isn't that the store where Leo bought me my sweater?" Gran asked.

"It is," Odelia said, suddenly getting a strange sensation in the pit of her stomach. "Can I take a look, Mom?" she asked.

"It's beautiful, Tex," Mom gushed. "Thank you so much."

Odelia took the blouse and checked the wash care label.

"What are you looking for, honey?" Tex asked with a laugh. "It's the genuine article, if that's what you're concerned about."

"I know it's the genuine article, Dad," she said, her grandmother looking on excitedly. "Just that…" She poked at the label, trying to see if something was hidden inside. And then she saw it. She dug her finger in and removed a small piece of paper, ripping it from the seam that had held it inside the label.

"What's that?" asked her dad, his smile disappearing.

She placed it on the table, and they all leaned in to see. The label said, 'HELP US! WE PRISONERS HERE!'

CHAPTER 15

The next morning, Dooley and I decided to go out and do some more sleuthing. We both felt that with all that was going on, we'd neglected our sacred duty to Odelia to do all we could to help her solve this celebrity chef's murder. The drama with Diego and Brutus had momentarily distracted us, but no more!

Unfortunately the drama hadn't abated. Harriet and Diego had eloped. They hadn't been home all night, and Dooley was starting to worry. I didn't, since I knew that Harriet could take care of herself. Besides, I hadn't forgotten how she kept hounding me to be BFFs with Brutus, and now suddenly she'd completely lost interest in the cat herself.

Well, two could play that game. I'd lost interest in her. Frankly, I felt betrayed. Harriet knew how we felt about Diego. In the rare moment we'd had her all to ourselves, we'd made it perfectly clear. And still she decided to run with the cat. Well, as far as I was concerned, she was on her own.

"Let's go, Brutus," I said, after chomping down a final piece of kibble.

We'd taken the big cat under our wing. After much

debate, we figured we couldn't simply let him hang around the house and be miserable. Better to get him out and about, helping the investigation along. I was sure it would do him a world of good. Besides, I hadn't lied. There were plenty of other female felines in the world. Maybe one would catch Brutus's eye and he'd forget all about that treacherous Harriet.

"Do I have to?" Brutus asked morosely.

"Yes, you do," I said. "No use moping. You need to move past this."

"But what if Harriet comes home, looking for me? I won't be here."

"She won't come home looking for you," I said. And when Dooley gave me the angry look again, I added, "Better to get the truth out there, buddy. Harriet won't be home anytime soon. So you better forget all about her and that Diego."

At the sound of his rival's name, a dark look came over Brutus's face. Yeah, I know it's hard to see with a black cat like Brutus, but trust me. The dark look came. It was there. "I never want to hear that name again," he said with a low growl.

"Sure. Let's just call him... Ivan, shall we?"

"Why Ivan?" asked Dooley, curiously.

"Why not? It's a name."

"Let's call him He Who Cannot Be Named," Brutus suggested.

"Isn't that a little dramatic?" I asked. "I mean, really?"

"Isn't that from a movie?" Dooley asked. "Something with stars. Um, *Star Trek*? No! Um, *Star Wars*! Or... *Starman*? *Stardust*!"

"Harry Potter, Dooley," I said curtly. "And no, we're not naming Diego He Who Cannot Be Named."

At the sound of the name Diego, Brutus had squeezed his

eyes shut and had started singing, "Lalalalalalal!" at the top of his voice. Very mature.

"Let's just ignore him altogether," Dooley said, very wisely in my opinion.

"Let's go, Brutus!" I cried.

He stopped singing Lalala and got up with a weary groan.

We left the house and set paw for the Hampton Springs Hotel. It wasn't all that far. Hampton Cove is pretty much a one-horse town. Well, actually it's a no-horse town, though we have many cats, as I've amply illustrated.

"So where are we going?" Brutus asked, as despondent as ever. "Not that I care," he added. "'Cause I don't. I just don't want to go too far. I'm feeling weak."

"Hey, I was feeling weak yesterday," Dooley said. "But that's because I thought I was dying. But then Odelia told me I was fine, and since she's a doctor, she can tell if you're dying, and I'm not, so now I'm fine again, if you see what I mean."

"What are you talking about?" Brutus grumbled. "Odelia is a reporter, not a doctor."

Uh-oh. I tried to gesture to the black cat, but he studiously ignored me.

"Odelia's dad is a doctor, and since that kind of stuff runs in the family, she's a doctor, too. It's all genetics, isn't that right, Max?"

I gave him my best smile and nodded. "Uh-huh."

"What a load of nonsense," Brutus said. "Doctors have to go to school for about a hundred years. That stuff's not genetic. It's taught! Odelia is as much a doctor as I am a voodoo priest. I'm not a voodoo priest," he added, to make things perfectly clear.

Dooley got that confused look in his eyes again. He gets that a lot. You might say it's his standard expression. "Max? What is Brutus saying?"

"Don't listen to Brutus. He's still thinking about Diego."

"Lalalalalala!" Brutus immediately sang.

"See? The guy doesn't know what he's saying," I said. "Trust me, Dooley. Odelia is a doctor and you're not going to die."

His face cleared again, and morphed into an expression of childlike glee. It's his second standard expression. All in all Dooley is pretty limited in his facial expressions.

"So where are we going?" Brutus asked again, once he'd caught on to the fact that I'd stopped using the name Diego.

We were ambling along the sidewalk and had already reached the end of the block. Only a few more blocks and we were at our destination.

"We're going to the Hampton Springs Hotel," Dooley informed him, a spring in his step. "We're going to see a dog about an alibi."

"Huh?" Brutus asked. "Did you say we're going to see a dog?"

"Yep. That's right. We're going to see Stacie Roebuck's dog Puck."

"Who's Stacie Roebuck and who's Puck?"

I sighed. That's what happens when you don't pay attention. "Stacie Roebuck is—or was—Niklaus Skad's assistant. It has come to our attention that Niklaus Skad owns—or owned—a Portuguese Water Dog."

"He's in all the pictures," said Dooley. "And was the mascot of *Kitchen Disasters*. That dog went everywhere with Niklaus."

"And according to Odelia, Stacie took the dog when Niklaus died."

"Portuguese Water Dogs are just the coolest, don't you think?" Dooley asked. "President Obama had a Portuguese Water Dog. He was called Bo. I like the name Bo. It's a nice name."

"What is this? *Jeopardy*? Who cares who had what dog called whatever? They're dogs—we're cats. We don't mingle."

"That's a very conservative point of view," I said. "It is my opinion that dogs can actually be very nice. I mean, dumb, of course—that stands to reason—but they can be very useful witnesses in a murder investigation. Remember that French bulldog we met not so long ago? The one that belonged to the dead reality star?"

"Oh, you mean Kane?" asked Dooley. "Yeah, he was nice, wasn't he?"

"Just a dumb mutt," Brutus muttered.

"Well, that dumb mutt provided us with the telling clue, didn't he?"

"He sure did, Max," Dooley said happily.

Brutus gave Dooley a dirty look. "Do you have to be so happy?"

"I'm not dying," Dooley said. "And that makes me happy as a clam!"

"Ugh," Brutus grunted, and shook his head. "You make me sick."

We arrived at the hotel and looked up at the third floor, where Odelia had told us Stacie Roebuck's room was. I hadn't worked out the logistics of this thing, and now saw the fatal flaw in my plan. How were we ever going to get up there?

"Um, how are we going to get up there, Max?" Dooley asked.

"Maybe we can jump," Brutus said, his words dripping with sarcasm.

"Why don't we just, you know, use the stairs?" I asked.

"You mean go inside?" Dooley asked. "What a novel idea! Max, you're so smart!"

And immediately he skipped away, en route to the hotel entrance.

"I swear, if he keeps this up I'm going to kill him," Brutus growled.

"Just leave him be," I said. "Dooley has a bipolar streak. Happy one minute, down the next."

"Don't tell me, did Doctor Odelia tell you this, too?" he snarled.

I shrugged. "Anything to keep him happy. I'm sure he's healthy, and now he believes it, too. So what's wrong with that?"

"What's wrong with that is that you lied to him."

"Just a little white lie."

"White lie or not, he'll find out soon enough, and he'll never believe you again."

I grinned. "Then you don't know Dooley. He has the memory span of a kitten. This time tomorrow he'll have forgotten all about this episode."

"Lucky him. I wish I could forget about Harriet and... You Know Who."

"Diego will not be a part of our lives for very long, Brutus," I said, and for once he didn't start singing Lalala but merely gave me a penetrating look.

"You better not be lying to me, Max. Cause I'm not like Dooley. I have a great memory. And if you're lying to me..." He heaved his paw and extended his claws. I swear they looked like something from *The Wolverine*. Sharp and long!

He didn't have to say more. I gulped. "I'm not lying," I promised, and I almost believed it myself.

"Come on, you guys!" Dooley yelled. "Try to keep up!"

We jogged after him, and up the few steps that led to the hotel entrance. It was one of those revolving doors and I didn't like the look of it. A cat can easily get stuck between those doors and be chopped in half!

"Um, I don't know if this is such a good idea," I ventured.

"It's a great idea!" Dooley said. "Just like a merry-go-round!" And before I could stop him, he'd darted up to the door and was streaking inside.

I shared a weary look with Brutus, and we both shook our heads. "Let's just do this," he grunted. Brutus went first, and I followed a close second. There was a momentary confusion when I had no idea if I'd missed my exit, but when I found myself in a plush-looking lobby, my claws digging into a nice high-pile burgundy carpet, I knew I was in the right place.

Dooley was already high-tailing it to the sweeping dual staircase, and lucky for us there weren't many people in the lobby, so no one stepped on my tail or kicked me in the ribs. Yep, the life of a cat can be brutal.

We hopped up the stairs, making great time, and found ourselves on the third floor without incident. Now to find the right room—and get inside!

"So which room is it?" asked Brutus, seeming to have perked up. A little adventure had done him a world of good. I swear he was already starting to forget all about Harriet and Diego.

"According to Odelia, Stacie is staying in room three-twenty-seven," I said, checking the numbers on the doors.

The carpeting in this hotel was very nice, and I couldn't resist digging my claws in for a moment and kneading it, sending clumps of carpet flying all around. Brutus and Dooley did the same. What? You can't fight instinct.

We arrived at Room 327 and plunked down on our haunches, staring at the closed door.

"Now what?" Brutus asked.

"Maybe we knock?" Dooley suggested.

"Yeah, why don't we knock? She'll let us in and maybe even give us a can of chicken liver," Brutus sneered.

"Do you really think so?" Dooley asked excitedly. He likes chicken liver.

"Of course not, you dumb-ass!"

And just like that, the old Brutus was back.

Suddenly, the door to Room 326 opened and an older man came shuffling out, leaning on a walker. I gave Dooley a glance and he nodded. So we quickly scooted over and slipped inside.

"Hey, wait for me!" Brutus yelled.

I held the door for him and he moved inside cautiously, his ears up and his whiskers trembling, ready for action. Immediately, I moved to the window and walked out onto the balcony. Phew. We were in luck. The balconies connected. So I hopped up onto the balustrade and made the smooth jump to the next balcony, then down to the floor and I was in!

Dooley and Brutus followed my lead, and then the three of us sat staring at the sliding door to Stacie Roebuck's room. Behind it, a very big, very hairy black dog sat staring at us, looking completely flabbergasted.

We'd found Puck.

CHAPTER 16

*P*uck stared at us. We stared at Puck. This was one of those *The Good, the Bad and the Ugly* type of situations. I had no idea who I was in this constellation. Definitely not the ugly one, and definitely not the bad one either. I think I was Clint. Yeah, definitely Clint.

The dog barked once, and I saw that the window was open a crack. Not a big crack, mind you. Big enough for us cats to slip inside, but not big enough for Puck to join us on the balcony.

"Um... so now what?" Dooley asked.

"Yeah, how do we know this yapper isn't homicidal?" Brutus asked.

I glanced down, and saw that I had a clear view of the pool down below. People were already prancing around, splashing in the pool. I wondered if Stacie was home. If she was, she might object to three cats entering her room. Then I had the bright idea of asking, "Is. Stacie. Home?"

I enunciated very clearly, cause I know from experience that dogs aren't the smartest species.

The dog barked again, and I took it as a sign that Stacie

was home. Then he became more eloquent. "She's in bed. She had a rough day yesterday and she's sleeping in."

"Thanks for making that clear," I said, still speaking slowly and clearly.

Puck frowned. "So why are you yelling, buddy?"

"I thought you might have trouble grasping my meaning."

"I'm grasping your meaning just fine. There's nothing wrong with my ears. Why don't you come in?"

I hesitated. This could be a trap. Then again, no dog has ever been able to catch a cat. We're built for speed, they're built to lumber along on a leash.

I put one paw forward, and Dooley asked, panicked, "You're not going in, are you, Max?"

"Why not? He doesn't look dangerous to me."

We stared at the dog, who gave us a dumb grin. "I know what this is," he said. "Candid camera, right? Am I being punked? Huh? Is that what this is?"

"Yeah, he's not dangerous," Brutus decided, and beat me inside. I went in second, with Dooley a close third.

The room was nice, in a generic hotel sort of way. These places all look the same to me. It was a small room, nothing fancy. Niklaus definitely hadn't splurged on his assistant's travel budget. He probably stayed in the suite, while Stacie had to make do with the crumbs.

"So we're investigating the murder of your human," I said. "Niklaus?"

"Yeah, I know who my human is," said Puck. "I mean, was."

He didn't look too broken up about the chef's death. "So what do you think happened?" I asked.

"Not so fast, Max," said Dooley. "You can't just waltz in here and start asking a bunch of questions." He nodded at Puck. "Hi, my name is Dooley, and these are Max and Brutus. We live with a woman named Odelia Poole. She's a reporter investigating the murder of your human. And we're here to help her."

"I've heard about you," said Puck. "Your human can communicate with you, right?"

"Where did you hear that?" Brutus immediately asked.

"There was a cat at the restaurant Niklaus was doing, um… what was her name again? Oh, that's right. Montserrat. She kinda belonged to one of the girls that worked there. She told me about this cat that talks to his human, and helps her solve murders and stuff. Max. That's you, right?"

"Yeah, that is me," I admitted, starting to swell a little with pride. So I was famous, huh? Cool.

"Did she also talk about me?" Dooley asked. "Cause we're buds, Max and I. We solve all these murders together."

"And don't forget about me," Brutus chimed in. "We're a trio now."

"Nah. She only mentioned Max. Said you were a big orange cat."

"Blorange," I was quick to correct him. "Yes, it's a color," I added before he could ask. "So what about Stacie? Do you think she killed Niklaus?"

"Max!" Dooley cried. "You can't just spring a question like that on him! Can't you see the dog is grieving?"

"I'm not grieving," said Puck, his soft brown eyes mellow and bright. He'd plunked his big, hairy body down and was resting his head on his front paws. He had a funny-looking white fringe that hung over his eyes. The guy clearly needed a trim.

"You're not?" Dooley asked. "But your human died."

"Yeah, and I'm happy he did. He was a pretty lousy human. Stacie is a great person, and so much nicer to me than Niklaus ever was. Did you know he used to beat me? Yeah, that's right. He was one of those humans. A nasty one."

"That's just terrible!" Dooley cried. "He beat you? How awful!"

"He treated Stacie pretty badly, too. Used to yell at her all the time. She used to cry a lot, but only when no one was watching. Except me. So I guess you could say we went through the same ordeal and came out the other end."

"You have a shoulder to cry on and so does she," Dooley said. "How moving."

"Are you crying, little buddy?" asked Puck.

"No," said Dooley in a strangled voice. "Just a speck of dust."

"Don't cry for us," said Puck. "We're great now. Stacie has already told me she plans to keep me, so I'm in dog heaven right now. Stacie is the best."

"So..." I glanced at Dooley, wondering if now was the time to ask the question. But he was so busy wiping his eyes that he didn't notice. I shrugged. "So did Stacie kill Niklaus?"

"Max!" Dooley cried.

"Yeah, Max," Brutus growled. "Where are your manners?"

"Hey, how else am I going to get an answer?"

"It's all right," said Puck. "The short answer is that I have no idea. I wasn't there when Niklaus was killed. He'd locked me up in his suite as usual. The long answer is that I'm pretty sure Stacie would never do such a thing. She's far too sweet. Besides, have you seen Stacie?"

"Um, no, we haven't," I said.

"She's small, buddy. And from what I hear the killer hoisted Niklaus all the way up into the restaurant oven." He shook his head, his fringe swishing. "Nah. No way that girl has the body strength to perform such a feat."

Well, I had my answer, and I was glad. Another suspect scratched from the list. Odelia would be happy.

"So do you have any idea who did kill Niklaus?" Brutus asked.

Great question. Why didn't I think of that?

His big, mellow dog eyes grew moist. "No idea. But whoever did it deserves a medal. Without him—or her—I would still be locked up in that suite, and Stacie would still be the least-appreciated assistant in the world."

It was pretty clear to me that Niklaus Skad's killer had done the world a favor, or at least Puck and Stacie. It was a touching story, and one I just knew would one day make a great Lifetime movie featuring Danica McKellar in the role of Stacie and Rob Lowe as Niklaus Skad. I wondered who'd play the dog. Or me!

Puck was recalling some more moving moments from his life as a dog, while Dooley listened with bated breath, Brutus checked out Puck's bowl for scraps, and I checked out the room for clues to Stacie's personality.

Suddenly the doorbell rang, and a tired voice sounded in the bedroom. "Who is it?!"

Then the voice of Odelia came through the door, loud and clear. "Odelia Poole, Miss Roebuck. Could I please have a moment of your time?"

CHAPTER 17

Odelia knocked on the door again. Maybe Stacie wasn't going to let her in? That was the disadvantage of being a reporter. Oftentimes people simply didn't allow you in. And she couldn't force them. It wasn't as if she was the police or something. No one was under any obligation to talk to her.

"Coming!" the same voice sounded from inside.

The door was opened and a tired-looking young woman looked out at her. "Yes?"

"Hi. Miss Roebuck? Miss Stacie Roebuck? My name is Odelia Poole? I'm a reporter with the Hampton Cove Gazette. I also work as a consultant with the Hampton Cove Police Department. I was wondering if I could ask you a few questions about your boss."

Stacie nodded and opened the door wider. As Odelia stepped in, she saw three cats and a dog sitting on the carpet staring up at her. She did a double take, and when she looked again, she saw that Max, Dooley and Brutus had vanished, and that only the dog was left. He was a big, black, hairy dog with soulful eyes.

"Lemme just close the window," said Stacie, and padded over barefoot, snapping it shut. Just before she did, Odelia saw how her three cats had been inching toward the window, which was probably how they'd gotten in in the first place. So now they were trapped. Great. Just great.

"I'm sorry to bother you at such an early hour," she said.

"No, that's all right. I must have overslept. Usually I get up at the crack of dawn, but now, with all that's happened, I guess I was just bone-tired last night."

Stacie Roebuck was a slight woman of around Odelia's age. She had half-long auburn hair and was wearing green-framed glasses, accentuating the jade in her eyes. There were also dark rims under those same eyes, adding substance to her words that she was indeed bone-tired. Which didn't surprise Odelia.

"Don't mind the mess," Stacie said apologetically. "It's been a hectic couple of days, as you can imagine."

Odelia looked around the room but saw no mess to speak of. Through the open door of the bedroom she could see some clothes strewn around in there, but the living room was perfectly spotless, which told her Stacie hadn't been in much. A laptop was open on the desk, and a neat pile of cookbooks—all authored by Niklaus Skad—were stacked next to the laptop, but otherwise there was absolutely no clutter.

The dog came over to her and pressed his nose into her hand. "He's sweet," she said with a smile. "Is he yours?"

"He is now," said Stacie with a tired smile. "His name is Puck, and he belonged to Niklaus. I've decided to adopt him."

"I'm sorry to have to ask you this," she said, "but do you have any idea what happened?"

Stacie shook her head. She was dressed in a purple sweater and sweatpants and sat at the edge of the sofa, Odelia right across from her. "I hadn't seen Niklaus since that morning. He'd done a taping at the restaurant and then decided he needed the day off. He said he'd spend it at the pool, or maybe at the beach, so I knew not to bother him."

"Did you also take the day off?"

"Oh, no," said Stacie with a laugh. "Niklaus hardly ever let me take the day off. There was always something that needed to be done."

"So what did you do?" asked Odelia, hoping her line of questioning wasn't too abrupt. She sometimes wished she had her uncle's flair for asking the right questions. He had a knack for putting people at ease.

"I stayed at the restaurant, setting up the next taping." She gestured with her hand. "There were some fires to put out—the chef..." Her voice trailed off, as she was aware there were certain things better left unsaid in front of a reporter.

"I'm not going to print any of this," Odelia said, "if you don't want to. What I want most of all is to find out what happened—who did this to Niklaus."

The assistant nodded. "Niklaus Skad wasn't the easiest man to work for. He had a habit of rubbing people the wrong way. It was his style—the thing he was known for—and the main reason people watched the show. They liked the abrasiveness. And the drama. The conflict and the outbursts. The way he humiliated people." She paused, bringing a trembling hand to her face, ineffectually pushing at her hair and then dropping it in her lap.

"I know this is hard for you," Odelia said, scooting forward.

"It's fine. It's just... There was a huge row during the taping, so I spent a big chunk of the day trying to put out the fire. The chef was so undone he told everyone he'd quit, and the owners were threatening to pull out of the show. It didn't help matters that I had to point out to them they'd signed a contract and that they couldn't cancel even if they wanted to."

"Looks like Niklaus liked to stir the pot and left you to pick up the pieces."

"That's exactly what he did."

"That can't have been much fun."

"No, it wasn't." She glanced at Puck, who'd put his head in her lap and was gazing up at her with his sad dog eyes. She placed a hand on the dog's head and smiled. "I think it's safe to say that neither me or Puck are very sorry that Niklaus is gone." She looked up in alarm. "Oh, I'm sorry. I shouldn't have said that. That was massively unprofessional of me."

"No, it's fine," said Odelia. "I've heard the stories. I've seen the shows. It must have been tough on you."

"Yes, it was. Probably the hardest job I've ever had. And the longest three years of my life."

"You worked for him for three years?"

Stacie nodded. "Everybody said I was crazy to stay. All his other assistants had walked out after only a couple of months —or weeks. But there was something special about Niklaus Skad. He might have been a demanding boss—and not a very nice one—but I admired him for what he'd achieved. He built an entire empire—a complete brand—all by himself and in record time. I couldn't help but have a lot of respect for him as a businessman. As a person? Not so much." She tickled Puck behind the ears. "For one thing, he wasn't very nice to Puck. And I resented that. Humans can defend themselves, but dogs can't."

"I agree," she said. "I hate people who are mean to animals."

"Me, too," said Stacie with a sad smile. "I just can't tolerate them."

"So… where were you when Mr. Skad died, Stacie? I'm sorry—I have to ask."

"Of course. I was right here, preparing for the next day's shoot. That's what I usually did at night. Making sure that everything was ready for the next day. So that Niklaus just had to walk on set and do his thing."

"Can anyone confirm that you were here?"

"Nope. Not even Puck. He was still locked up in Mr. Skad's suite." She gave Odelia a hesitant look. "Do you think the police will suspect me?"

"I think you'll be one of the suspects, yes."

She nodded. "Of course. I had the motive to kill him. And I certainly had opportunity. Though I had no idea he returned to the restaurant. Usually when we were out on location he liked to stay in his room and…" She grimaced. "… invite company."

"Female company?"

"Yes. He liked to go out and, well, sample the local offerings."

"Why do you think he went back to the restaurant? Maybe he wanted to prepare for the next day?"

She shook her head adamantly. "No way. Niklaus never bothered with that. He even told me once he stayed far away from the restaurants he was doing. He wanted to arrive on the scene with fresh eyes and go with his gut. He didn't want to overthink things. Visiting a restaurant the night before a shoot was something he'd never do."

"So you have no idea why he returned?"

"None."

She eyed the woman curiously. She was slight. Too slight to be able to lift the body of her boss up and into the oven. If she were the murderer she would have needed help. No way she could have done this alone. "Thank you, Stacie."

"You're welcome. I suppose the police will want a word with me?"

"Yes, I'm afraid they will. But don't worry. My uncle is a kind and fair man."

"Your uncle is a policeman?"

"Yes. He's Chief of Police."

They both rose, and Stacie stood hugging herself for a moment. "I hope he catches whoever did this. I would like to go home and put this whole thing behind me as soon as possible."

"I'm sure we'll catch the culprit soon," she said, projecting a confidence she wasn't exactly feeling. So far they had nothing. Unless this Chef Serarols proved to be a viable suspect. Her uncle certainly seemed to think so. "What was your impression of Hendrik Serarols?"

"He seemed nice enough. I think he's a great chef, and he only made those mistakes because Niklaus was giving him such a hard time. It's not easy to perform under such great pressure." She gave a weak smile. "I speak from experience." Her smile vanished. "Why? Do you think he did it?"

"He doesn't have an alibi for the night of the murder, so…"

"I can't believe he would do such a thing. But then again, I guess everybody is capable of murder, even the ones you least suspect."

"That is certainly true," she agreed.

From the corner of her eye, she saw that Max was frantically trying to get her attention. So she walked to the door and opened it, then blocked Stacie's view of it by pointing at the window. "Is it true that Niklaus Skad's wife gave such a performance the night her husband was killed?"

Stacie grinned. "Oh, yes, she did. I honestly couldn't watch. It was so embarrassing. A woman like her pouncing on a man half her age? There was something really tragic about it."

She watched as Max, Dooley and Brutus snuck out through the door. "You knew her well? Cybil Truscott?"

"I did. And I'd say Niklaus and Cybil deserved each other. They were both people who only cared about themselves." Puck gave a bark of agreement at this, and Stacie bent down and gave him a hug. "This guy here is just about the only good thing I'm taking away from this experience."

"He's lucky to have you," Odelia said.

"No, I'm lucky to have him," Stacie said.

And as she stepped out and closed the door behind her, she was convinced that Stacie was innocent. No way anyone could fake that performance.

She looked around, and saw that Max and the others were waiting for her at the top of the stairs. "What were you guys doing in there?" she asked, crouching down.

"You told us to have a talk with Puck, so we did," Max said simply.

"And? What's the verdict?"

"Puck doesn't think Stacie could have done it. She's way too sweet."

"And too weak," Brutus added.

"Too slight," Max corrected him.

"I agree," Odelia said. "I don't think she did it."

"So who did?" Dooley asked.

"If you can answer that, I'll give you all the chicken wings you could ever dream of," she said, giving Dooley a pat on the head.

The cat grinned. "See, Brutus? That power of the mind thing is working already!"

CHAPTER 18

e plodded down the stairs in Odelia's wake. I was feeling pretty exhilarated. This mission had been a success. I actually felt like James Bond or something: sneaking into hotel rooms to spy secrets and stuff. The only difference between James and me was that there hadn't been a pretty girl waiting in that hotel room but a big, hairy dog. Story of my life, I guess.

"So what's next?" Brutus asked. The mission had cheered him up.

"Next is that we need to get rid of this Diego character," I said.

Brutus shook his head. "It can't be done, Max. Didn't you hear Odelia? He's here to stay."

"Not if you make him go away," I said.

"Me? How can I make him go away?"

"You just have to put your paw down, Brutus. You have to lay it all out for him. You have to show him who's the boss."

He paused halfway down the stairs. "And how am I supposed to do that?"

"The same way you showed us who's boss," I said.

"Remember when you first arrived in town? How you told us you were the cat of a cop and you were laying down the law from now on and a bunch of little sissy cats weren't going to stand in the way of you achieving world domination?"

"Um, I don't think that's what happened," Dooley said.

"It's how I remember it," I said. "And that's what counts. What it all comes down to is that you have to cat up, Brutus. Girls like a strong cat. A cat who tells it like it is. Who takes no crap from no one, and definitely not from some nasty skinny-ass cat like Diego."

Throughout my little pep talk, Brutus was perking up. He was almost looking like his old self again. Whether this was a good thing or not remained to be seen. I was pumping him up. Boosting his ego. He might just as easily turn against us. Side with Diego and make our lives a living hell. But I didn't think so. We had an actual opportunity here to make Brutus our ally and not our enemy and we had to take it. The enemy of my enemy is my friend, or something along those lines. And since Diego was clearly the bigger of two evils here, Brutus needed to become our friend.

"For once I think you're right, Max," Brutus said, his eyes displaying a malevolent gleam. "For once I think you might be right on the money."

I didn't like this 'for once' nonsense. In my humble opinion I was always right. But I wasn't going to let a little thing like that ruin the moment. "You have to waltz in there and take back your sweetheart," I said.

"Wait, what?" asked Dooley.

"You have to simply grab her and plant a big, wet one on her lips and tell her that daddy's home and no one is going to take her away from you."

"Um, Max?" Dooley asked. "What are you doing?"

"I'm going to squash that little pipsqueak like a bug!"

Brutus growled. "I'm going to storm in there and take my girl back from that… that… nincompoop!"

"Well said," I said, putting my paws together for an impromptu applause.

"And I'm going to do it right now!" Brutus said.

"No time like the present," I agreed.

"I'm going to bulldoze that crappy cat into the ground!"

"I love the sentiment," I said with genuine admiration.

And Brutus stalked off. "Watch me going!" he shouted.

"I'm watching you going and I'm inspired!" I shouted back.

Both Dooley and I watched Brutus storm down the hotel steps, into the lobby and out that treacherous revolving door.

"Max!" cried Dooley the moment the big brute was out of earshot. "What have you done?!"

I smiled. "I've handled two problems in one stroke of genius, Dooley. I've turned an enemy into an ally, and I've rid ourselves of this annoying Diego. Don't congratulate me now. You can do that when all this is over."

"I'm not going to congratulate you! Brutus was down, and now you've gone and boosted him all up again!"

"I know, right. Isn't it great?"

"No, it's not! He's going to kick Diego out of the house."

"Which is what we want, remember?"

"And then he's going to turn on us!"

I gave this some thought. "No, he's not. He's our friend now."

"Brutus is nobody's friend! A cat like that can't be friends with anybody. He's like Niklaus Skad. Stepping on people and putting them down makes him feel good. Once he's done stepping on Diego who do you think he's going to step on next?"

"Um, nobody? Because he'll be happy that Diego's gone

and he's got Harriet back and he's going to be grateful to his new best friends. Us!"

"No, he's not! He's going to keep putting cats down. He's going to kick us out next!"

"No way. We're his friends. We stood by his side when he was down and out."

"It doesn't work like that, Max. He's going to feel embarrassed because we saw him when he was down. He's going to want to take revenge. He's going to come down harder on us than on anyone else." He closed his eyes. "This is the end. You just created a monster and set him loose on us."

"I don't think you're right, Dooley," I said, though I had to admit he made a very convincing argument. It was true that bullies like Brutus hate to look weak. And we'd seen him at his weakest. At his lowest. We'd even seen him—gasp!—cry. Now that he was strong again—and boosted by the victory over Diego—he just might become fully insufferable. And vindictive.

"We watched him weep, Max. He's never going to forgive us."

"Let's just wait and see," I said. "I'm sure he'll be just fine. Tonight we'll all be sitting on the couch. Odelia, you, me, Brutus and Harriet, watching a great movie, and having a laugh about all of this. All friends together, right?"

He merely shook his head.

"Right? Dooley?"

He stared at me with accusing eyes. "What have you done, Max?"

CHAPTER 19

*O*delia crossed the lobby to the door, lost in thought. That's why she didn't notice Chase until she bumped into him and almost went down. He placed two steadying hands on her shoulders. "Hold your horses, honey. Are you all right?"

The impact had done much to make her aware of the hardness of his chest and the power of his hands. The man was made of solid rock! "Um, yes, I'm fine," she said, a little flustered. She made an effort to control her beating heart as she stepped away from him. "I wasn't looking."

"That's what I figured," he said with a hint of a smile. "I'm here to interview another suspect. You?"

"Same thing," she said. "I just had a chat with Stacie Roebuck."

"The assistant? What did she have to say?"

"She was alone the night her boss died. Holed up in her room."

"No alibi, huh?"

"Nope. None, whatsoever. Though I don't think she did it. You should see her, Chase. She's this sweet, slim woman."

He cocked an eyebrow. "Incapable of shoving a two-hundred-and-fifty-pound male into an oven?"

"I don't think she could have done it. And not just physically. She might have disliked her boss—"

"He seemed to have had that effect on a lot of people."

"—but she respected him for what he'd achieved."

"All right," he said. "And I respect your judgment." He hesitated. "Why don't you join me?"

"Interviewing a suspect? But I'm not a cop."

"You're practically deputized," he said. "And it's not like we haven't done it before."

That was true enough. They'd interviewed other suspects before. She hadn't lied to Stacie. Uncle Alec had given her a consultant status some time back, when he realized she could be a boon to his investigations. That still didn't mean she could sit in on interrogations at the precinct. She could, however, tag along when a detective like Chase talked to witnesses and interviewed suspects. Like Rick Castle shadowing Kate Beckett.

"So who are you interviewing?" she asked as she fell into step beside him.

"There's this guy who was one of Niklaus Skad's main competitors. He's a former chef who now has a cooking show on NBC. It was scheduled to go head to head with *Kitchen Disasters* and to everyone's surprise managed to get more viewers than anyone thought."

CHAPTER 20

"Ooh! I think I know him. Konrad Daines, right? *Chopped Liver?*"

"Yeah, that's the one. You know your cooking shows, Odelia."

"I always hope to pick something up."

"I have to confess I'd never heard of the guy. Or Niklaus Skad, for that matter. But then I'm not much of a cook."

"Me neither," she confessed. "I just figure that maybe by watching a lot of cooking shows I'll become a master chef."

"You mean by osmosis?"

"Yep. That's exactly what I mean. Silly, huh?"

"Nah. It's like guys watching football. They just sit there with their beer bellies, totally out of shape, and somehow figure that if they watch enough games some of that athleticism just might rub off on them. Human nature, I guess."

"Or laziness."

He grinned. "Or that."

They walked back to the main staircase, and she noticed Max, Dooley and Brutus had vanished. Probably on the case, just like she and Chase were. "You watch a lot of football?"

He laughed. "What are you saying? That I'm a couch potato?"

She glanced him up and down. "No, you're definitely not a couch potato."

"Thanks. I try to stay in shape. Not football, mind you, but I do hit the gym on a semi-regular basis."

"I wish I could say the same."

"Why don't you join me? I could use a spotter."

Her eyebrows shot up. "Me? And you? Gym buddies?"

"Why not? It's a lot more fun when it's not just you and the treadmill."

"I don't know…" She pictured Chase hanging over her while she desperately tried to push up a huge barbell, veins standing out on her neck, breaking into a sweat. Not exactly the way she wanted to look in front of him. It was true that she needed to get in shape, though. Desperately so, in fact. And he definitely looked like a guy who knew his way around a gym.

"They've got separate dressing rooms if that's what you're worried about."

"Oh, I know they do. It's just…"

"You don't want me to see you in your gym clothes, huh? Is that it?"

"No! Of course not." Well, yes. She didn't want him to see her flabby midsection. Or her flabby tush. Or her flabby anything.

As if he could read her mind, he gave her a once-over. "I think you're in pretty great shape, actually. You probably don't even need to go to the gym."

"Oh, trust me, I do," she said. Then, before she could change her mind, added, "Fine. I'll be your gym buddy. But if you make one comment about my butt…"

"I might make a compliment about your butt," he said with a smirk.

"Yeah, right. Once you see my butt squeezed into spandex you'll wipe that smirk straight off your face."

"I think your butt looks great, with or without spandex."

"Are we really talking about my butt now?"

"You started it."

"You started it. I think."

They'd arrived on the second floor, and he checked his notebook. "Konrad Daines. Room twenty-four. Let's see if Mr. Daines is home, shall we?"

They traversed the hallway, passing a woman vacuuming the red carpeted floor and another dumping a bunch of linen into a trolley. They stopped in front of Room 24 and Chase knocked on the door.

"Did you ever get that chef to give up his alibi?" she asked.

"As a matter of fact I did. Turns out he was over at another restaurant in the next town for an interview. Was so sick and tired of Niklaus Skad that he was going to quit *Fry Me for an Oyster* and start work for the competition."

"And he didn't want to jeopardize his chances by blabbing about the interview."

"Exactly. So that's another suspect we can scratch from our list."

Just then, the door swung open, and an irate-looking man stood in the doorway. "Yes? What do you want?"

Chase held up his badge. "Hampton Cove Police Department, Mr. Daines. Detective Kingsley and this is Odelia Poole, civilian consultant. May we come in?"

The man's scowl instantly morphed into a look of concern. "Sure, sure. Is this about what happened the other night? My lawyer promised me he'd taken care of everything. That I was off the hook."

They stepped into the room, and Odelia noticed how it was a lot nicer than Stacie Roebuck's cramped quarters. There was a small foyer which opened up into a living room with an ocean view, a dining room and a kitchen. Two bedrooms led off the living room, one of which sported a four-poster bed.

The man led them into a salon and bade them take a seat. Odelia and Chase picked out a couple of chairs while Konrad settled himself on a settee.

"Actually we're here to talk about the murder of Niklaus Skad," Odelia said.

"Oh!" said the man. He was exactly as she remembered him from *Chopped Liver*. Barrel-chested with a tan even-featured face, bristly short hair, and keen eyes.

The show featured ten couples that were given the opportunity to open a pop-up restaurant. Undercover judges visited each restaurant and recorded their assessments, in no-holds-barred confession-cam style. Hidden cameras filmed the contestants as they responded to customer criticism and other crises. Tempers ran high, and when the teams reviewed their assessments at the end of each episode, typically lots of tears were shed and Kleenex doled out. The big prize was to open an actual restaurant.

"I take it you're aware that Niklaus Skad was killed?" Chase asked.

"Of course. Yes, I heard about that," said Konrad.

"You and Mr. Skad were competitors?" Odelia asked.

"Yes. Yes, we were. His *Kitchen Disasters* and my *Chopped Liver* were scheduled in the same time slot. His on Fox and mine on NBC."

"Is it true that your show was being axed at the end of its current season?" Odelia asked.

The man's face darkened. "So you read about that, huh? Yeah, it's true. It's also the reason for my little... incident the other night."

"Yes, let's talk about that," said Chase. "You said something about your lawyer promising you something? What's that all about?"

"Oh, um…" He looked sheepish now. "I thought that's why you guys were here. I had too much to drink and, well, I kinda passed out on the beach."

"You passed out on the beach?" Chase asked, jotting down a note.

"Yes, that's right. Right after I crashed Bill and Hillary's party."

"Bill and Hillary… as in Clinton?" asked Odelia, surprised.

Konrad heaved a deep sigh and settled back on the settee. "Not my finest hour, I must confess. You see, I'd just gotten the news about my show being canceled, and I wasn't in the best of moods. But instead of staying in my room, like I probably should have, I decided to go out and party. A buddy of mine has a yacht in one of the marinas in East Hampton, so I dropped by for a drink. Our company moved to the beach and we polished off a few bottles of bubbly." He paused, rubbing the back of his neck.

"And then?" Chase prompted.

"And then things got kinda vague. I remember sitting by a campfire listening to some dude playing the guitar. Then some of the girls wanted to go skinny-dipping and asked me if I was game. And I guess I was, cause next thing I remember I woke up in a prison cell and some cop accused me of crashing Bill's birthday party and making a nuisance of myself." He shrugged. "What happened between the skinny-dipping and the Clintons I don't know."

"And this all happened the night Niklaus Skad was killed?" Odelia asked.

"Yeah, you can check with East Hampton police. I was in jail when Niklaus was killed. First thing I heard about it was when my lawyer came to bail me out in the morning."

"I take it you and Mr. Skad didn't get along?" Chase asked.

"No, we most definitely didn't. That guy stole my idea. I was going to do a show called *Kitchen Calamities*. This was months before he pitched *Kitchen Disasters* to the networks. When I heard about it, I confronted him. He just laughed in my face. Said I shouldn't have blabbed about the concept to everyone I knew." He frowned. "Bastard didn't even deny stealing my idea. And then of course it made him a fortune and a household name."

It was obvious there was no love lost between the two celebrity chefs, but if his story about crashing the Clinton party was true, it would be easy to check. Which let him off the hook. "Do you have any idea who might have wanted to hurt Mr. Skad?" Odelia asked.

The man uttered a curt laugh. "Um, just about everybody? Niklaus wasn't a well-liked man, Miss Poole. He made a lot of enemies over the years, and worst of all, he was proud of the fact. Always said that the number of enemies a man had showed how successful he was. He even bragged about how hated he was."

Yep. That sounded about right.

"Thank you for your time, Mr. Daines," Chase finally said, after checking a few more things. "You've been most helpful."

The chef stood and shook Chase's hand. "No, I'm afraid I haven't. Look, I know you have to find the killer—it's your duty, after all—but let me tell you that most people you will talk to will tell you the same thing: they're all happy Niklaus was killed. That man was evil, Detective. Pure evil."

When they stepped from the room, Chase heaved a deep sigh. "So I guess that's it then. Another suspect down. We don't have any left."

"Poor man. First Skad stole his million-dollar idea for a

show, and then he went and got his own show canceled. He must have hated him so much."

"Yeah, he's the best suspect I've talked to so far. Physically he's also perfect. He could easily have shoved Skad into that oven. And he was in town the night of the murder."

"Pity he's got an ironclad alibi."

"Rock solid," Chase agreed.

"So where does that leave us?"

"We're still waiting on the final report from the coroner, but barring any surprises we're pretty much out of moves here. I honestly don't know who else could have done it."

"You talked to the rest of the staff?"

"All of them. They all alibied out."

"And no witnesses have come forward?"

"None. Which is weird, as someone must have seen something."

They descended the stairs, and Odelia gave the interview some more thought. Chase was right. Konrad was the perfect suspect. And he was innocent.

"Looks like you've got your work cut out for you, Detective Kingsley."

He gave her a grimace. "So now suddenly it's my investigation again, huh?"

"You are the detective. I'm just a consultant."

He shook his head. "Round about now we could use some of those magic sleuthing powers your uncle claims you possess. Cause from where I'm standing things are starting to look pretty hopeless."

She thought of Max and Dooley. If they didn't come up with something soon, Chase was absolutely right. Things did look hopeless.

CHAPTER 21

$\mathcal{A}$ ll the way back from the hotel to the house, I thought about what Dooley had said about Brutus. How I'd stirred the beast and he would return to haunt us. And when we were about to turn the corner and enter the street where we lived, I saw Brutus coming toward us, and he looked completely deflated again.

I nudged Dooley. "Look who's coming."

"He doesn't look like he's going to bully us," Dooley said.

"Very observant of you, Dooley. So maybe you were wrong, huh?"

"Let's wait and see."

"Hey, that's my line!"

"And now it's mine."

We sat down on our haunches, and I started casually licking my tail. I didn't want to give Brutus the impression we were waiting for him. Dooley, catching on, started licking his private parts.

"Dooley!" I hissed. "Do you have to do that now?"

"Huh? What?" he asked, looking up from his business.

"Just lick your paw or something. This is a public place."

"I don't have to lick my paw. I just licked my paw before. Now I want to lick my—"

"It's not proper!"

He stared at me. "What's gotten into you all of a sudden? We're cats, Max. Not humans. We lick whatever we want to lick at any given time."

"Still."

"Still nothing. Living with Odelia has turned you into a human. Time to remember that you're a cat."

I guess he was right. It's just that every time in the past I started licking my privates, Odelia started giggling. It's made me self-conscious.

"I honestly think that if people would walk around in the nude more and lick their private parts in public, the world would be a much better place," Dooley said.

I watched as Gran and Leo came walking down the street, kissing and hugging and generally all over each other's business, and I said, "I disagree. There are certain human private parts I really don't care seeing."

Brutus had reached us and also plunked down on his haunches. "Hi," he said in a tired voice. He sounded like the voice from the tomb on a bad day.

"So?" I asked. "How did it go?"

"It didn't. I waltzed in there, just like you told me to, and told Diego what was what. I said Harriet was my girlfriend and he had no right to come barging into our lives and stealing her away from me." He paused, and clamped his mouth shut, giving me a haunted look. Then he shivered visibly. "Brrrr."

"And?" I asked. "Don't keep us in suspense. What happened?"

"Harriet happened. She told me in no uncertain terms that she was no plaything, to be handed over from cat to cat and to be decided over by anyone but herself. She said she was her own cat and she was perfectly capable of deciding who she was going to date and I was an idiot for trying to control her." He shivered, and it was obvious the episode had rankled him.

"She said that, huh?"

"All that and a lot more," he admitted. "She also said that if she wanted to give her heart to Diego then that was nobody's business but her own. And if I thought I was going to change her mind by acting like a jealous boyfriend I had another thing coming. And then she kissed Diego. For about a minute or so. It could have been longer. I decided not to stick around."

I shared a look of commiseration with Dooley. The latter shrugged. He obviously figured that at least Brutus hadn't turned into the bullying monster we'd all come to know and despise. He was just his old, miserable self again.

I patted the big cat on the shoulder. "Why don't you join us, Brutus?"

"What are you doing?"

"I'm licking my tail and Dooley is licking his privates."

"Why not?" he asked, heaving another deep sigh. "It's not like I have anything better to do."

So we spent the next ten minutes grooming ourselves. It's an important part of being a cat, and it helps to take your mind off things.

"So what's new?" Brutus asked after a while.

"Nothing," I said.

"You think Odelia cracked the case yet?"

"Nope," I said.

"So what's our next move?"

I gave this some thought. What was our next move? The only thing I could come up with was to spend some time at our usual haunts. The barber shop. The police station. The General Store. Maybe someone somewhere had seen something and could get this investigation moving in the right direction again.

So once we were satisfied that our fur was all nice and shiny again and generally flea-free, we ambled off in the direction of Main Street. The police station was a bust. No cats around, and Uncle Alec was holed up in his office playing Solitaire on his computer. The barber shop was a bust, too. None of the cats hanging around there had seen anything.

Our final destination was the General Store, where our buddy Kingman reigns supreme. He's a large piebald that likes to gossip. And since just about every cat in town passes by the store eventually, he's usually the best choice to pick up some juicy fresh gossip.

"Max! Dooley! Brutus!" Kingman said from his perch on the counter. He likes to keep his human Wilbur company while the latter rings up the purchases. He gracefully hopped down and trod over to where we were sitting, right next to the discount DVD bin. "So what's happening, dudes?"

"We were just about to ask you," I said.

"Quid pro quo, Max," Kingman said with a sly grin. "Quid pro quo."

"Grandma Poole is dating a guy called Leo Wetland," I said.

He made a throwaway gesture with his paw. "That's old news. You'll have to do a lot better than that."

"Niklaus Skad was killed?" Dooley tried.

"Old news!"

I glanced at Brutus. He was sitting on the biggest piece of news. He shook his head. I gave him a penetrating look. He shook his head again. So I decided to blurt it out myself. "Harriet is dating a cat called Diego."

This time an eager look came into Kingman's eyes. "Tell me more."

So we told him more, Brutus meanwhile suffering the death of a thousand cuts. I told myself it was for a good cause. If Kingman wanted juicy gossip, it meant he had a big story to share, or else he wouldn't bother.

"Diego, huh? I've seen that cat around. Strutting his stuff. Bad news, Max. Bad news."

"Tell me something I don't know."

His eyes flashed. "Did you know that there's a sweatshop in town?"

"No way!"

"Yes, way. Right here in Hampton Cove. An actual sweatshop!"

"What's a sweatshop?" Dooley asked.

"It's a shop where people go to sweat," Brutus said.

"Like a fitness club?"

"Yeah, exactly like a fitness club," said Brutus. "Right, Max?"

"No, not like a fitness club," I said.

"So what is it?" asked Dooley, confused.

I gestured at Kingman. "You tell 'em."

"A sweatshop is a place where unscrupulous businessmen keep a bunch of workers—often even kids—and make them work really, really hard for pretty much no pay, for long hours and in horrible conditions."

"I knew that," I murmured, even though I didn't.

"I get it," Dooley said. "They make them sweat a lot and don't pay them anything."

"But isn't that, like, illegal?" Brutus asked.

"Good point, buddy!" said Kingman. "Of course it's illegal!"

"Yeah, they probably don't pay any taxes," I said.

"And they're breaking pretty much every labor law," Kingman added.

"So where is this sweatshop? And how do you even know this?"

"A cat that hangs out there told me. Said they've got a bunch of illegal aliens locked up in there."

"Aren't all aliens illegal?" asked Dooley. "I mean, I've seen *Independence Day*. Those horrible creatures definitely weren't invited."

"Not aliens from outer space," I said. "Aliens as in immigrants."

"Oh. Right," he said, understanding dawning.

"Norma said they look Chinese," said Kingman. "One of the workers actually feeds her milk from time to time. Through a crack in the window. She said there are bars on all the windows and they're not allowed outside."

"Terrible," Brutus said, and I could tell he was moved by the story. So was I. In this day and age, in this country, this was a real outrage.

"So where is this sweatshop?" I asked.

CHAPTER 22

*O*delia was hitching a ride in Chase's car when suddenly she saw three cats tripping along the sidewalk. They were Max, Dooley and Brutus. When Max spotted the car, he motioned for her to pull over.

"Pull over, Chase," she said. "Pull over right here."

"What's going on?" he asked, doing as she asked.

Without responding, she opened the door and allowed the three cats to hop in.

"Oh, God. Not your cats again," Chase said.

She ignored him. If Max signaled her to stop, he had something important to tell her.

"There's a sweatshop in town, Odelia," he said the moment he got into the car. "Kingman talked to Norma who said there are a lot of Chinese illegal aliens being kept on an old farm on the edge of town."

"They've got bars on the windows, Odelia," said Dooley.

"And they're not allowed to leave," said Brutus.

"And they have to work really hard," Max added.

She glanced over at Chase. "You're going to have to trust me on this, Chase."

137

He looked puzzled. "Trust you on what?"

"Remember when you said I should use my sleuthing magic to solve this case?"

"Uh-huh?"

"Well, this is me pulling the sleuthing magic card and telling you just to drive where I tell you to drive and not ask me any questions."

"Wait, what?"

She turned around, to the three cats who were now propped up on the backseat. "It's the old Tucker place, out on Dubarq Road," Max said.

"Go straight and then take a right at the end of the block," she told Chase.

*I*t didn't take them long to arrive at their destination. And even though Chase had thrown her a lot of curious glances, he'd managed to refrain from asking her any questions. Now that they were nearing their destination, he abruptly pulled the car onto the shoulder, cut the engine and turned to her.

"So what's this all about? What is back there at that old house?"

"It's an old farm, and... I think there's a sweatshop out there."

He stared at her. "A sweatshop. In Hampton Cove. And you know that how?"

Now came the tricky part. "You remember when I told you about the note Gran found in her new Ziv Riding sweater?"

"The cry for help, yes."

"And when Mom found a similar note in her blouse?"

"You think those notes came from this place?"

"Yes, I do. I think Ziv Riding isn't having his clothes

manufactured in Asia, like he claims. I think he's having them manufactured right here in Hampton Cove, only in appalling conditions by people who are being held here against their will, and forced to work in terrible circumstances."

He looked over the dashboard at the old farm. It didn't look like a sweatshop, but she knew that if Max told her there was a sweatshop out there, he was most likely right. Cats had ways of finding out stuff.

Chase rubbed his chin thoughtfully, then turned back to face her. "So how do you know?"

"I, um..." She glanced back at the cats through the rearview mirror. They were shaking their heads, No! "See, the thing is..."

"I'm listening," he said.

"I can't tell you," she finally said.

He uttered a surprised grunt. "What?"

"I simply can't tell you."

"That's ridiculous. Either you knew already about this sweatshop, and completely forgot about it until you saw your cats parading down the street, or somehow your cats told you about this sweatshop, which is completely ridiculous." He studied her for a moment. "So which is it, Odelia?"

She threw up her hands. "You're right. Silly me. I totally forgot about the sweatshop. Seeing Max and Dooley and Brutus brought it all back to me."

"Because..."

"Because..." She rooted around for a plausible response. "Because the person who called me last night and told me about the sweatshop also has a cat," she said finally. "And seeing Max and the others reminded me."

In the backseat, Max slapped his paw to his face. "Oh, God," he muttered.

"And you can't tell me who this person is?" Chase asked.

"I promised her I wouldn't reveal her identity."

He nodded, tapping his steering wheel. "Of course. And how did this person happen to find out?"

"She just happened to pass here the other day, and heard muffled shouts and cries. So she went to investigate closer and saw a bunch of people in there, locked up and being forced to sew Ziv Riding's clothes."

He gave her a comical grimace. "That's just about the most ridiculous story I've ever heard. But I'm willing to give you a pass, Odelia."

"You are? I mean, it's the honest-to-God's truth."

"Of course it is." He directed a suspicious look back at the cats. "I don't know what's going on here, but I'm going to hazard a guess it's got something to do with those cats. I don't know what it is but I'm not going to pressure you into telling me."

She blinked. "You're not?"

"No, I'm not. I guess when the time comes and you feel you can trust me, you'll tell me. For now I think our first priority should be to get those people out of there. But first we need to make sure your... source is telling the truth."

"My source never lies," she assured him.

He gave her a lopsided grin. "Honey, I'm a cop. Double-checking hot tips is what I do for a living. So please humor me."

"Sure," she said, pleasantly surprised that he'd let her off the hook so easily. "I'll come with you."

"No, that's all right. You better stay here and out of sight. We don't want to spook them and make them close up shop before we can get the cavalry out here."

He opened the door and got out. But before he did, she said, "Chase?"

He stuck his head back in. "What?"

She gave him a warm smile. "Thank you."

"Don't thank me yet. One of these days I'm going to get

you to spill all of your secrets, Odelia Poole. Just you wait and see."

"I'd like to see you try."

"Oh, but you will."

He gave the roof a pat and then he was off, keeping low, moving with surprising agility and grace. She saw him dart through a meadow, then he disappeared from sight.

"That was a close call," she said, heaving out a long breath.

"Are you going to tell him?" Max asked.

"Maybe one day," she said musingly. "But not now. Definitely not now."

"I think you should tell him," Brutus said surprisingly.

"And why is that?"

"There should be no secrets in a relationship," he said.

She laughed. "For your information, we're not in a relationship."

"You will be," he said.

"Don't mind Brutus," said Max. "He's feeling a little out of sorts on account of the fact that Diego stole his girlfriend."

"Diego stole Harriet?" she asked, surprised. "That was quick work."

"He's a quick worker," Max said.

"He's a snake," Brutus grunted. "A viper in your bosom, Odelia."

"Hey, watch what you say about Odelia's bosom," Dooley said.

"It's an expression," Max said.

"I don't care! Brutus better show some respect."

"I have the greatest respect for Odelia," said Brutus. "You took me in when my need was high."

"Your need wasn't high," said Dooley. "You got fed meat every day by Chase."

"Chase never feeds me any meat. He barely notices I'm

there. Chase is not a cat person. He just took me in because his mother asked him to."

Max and Dooley goggled at Brutus. "No meat?" asked Max.

"No juicy steak," Dooley asked.

"Just generic kibble," Brutus grunted. "The kind on sale in your local supermarket."

"Oh, Brutus," said Odelia, touched.

"Don't get me wrong," said Brutus. "I love Chase. But… I love Odelia more."

Silence reigned in the car for a few beats, then both Dooley and Max gave Brutus a hug, and Odelia reached back and tickled him under his chin. "And we love you, Brutus," Dooley assured him.

"Well, we do now," Max corrected him.

"Must have been that lack of meat that made him so intolerable," Dooley added.

"Thanks," Brutus grunted, clearly undone by these signs of affection. "Thanks, you guys. You're the best friends a cat can ever hope to get. I won't forget this."

"You're all right, Brutus," Odelia said. "I'll buy you all some meat tonight."

There was a tap on the roof of the car and they all jumped a foot in the air. Then Chase's head appeared through the open window. He was panting a little, and he was chewing on a piece of straw. "That's a sweatshop, all right. Let's call in the state police. This is a lot bigger than Hampton Cove." He glanced back at the cats. "Well done, you guys." He then directed a look at Odelia. "And now I'm talking to your cats. I'm going all screwy."

"Not screwier than Odelia," said Max.

Chase whipped his head around. "Was it my imagination or did he just talk back to me?"

But Odelia merely smiled.

CHAPTER 23

$\mathcal{W}$e patiently waited in the car until the state police that Chase had called in arrived. They came zooming down the road, blinkers and sirens off. The first car stopped right next to ours, and Chase quickly switched cars, and rode in with the cavalry. They surrounded the farmhouse. We watched from our first-row seat as dozens of cops exited their vehicles and descended upon the old Tucker farm, weapons drawn, approaching slowly and stealthily.

When finally Chase gave the all-clear sign, Odelia let us out of the car and we walked up with her.

We saw dozens of ill-dressed people being led out of the farmhouse. They looked unkempt and scared. Ambulances drove up and teams of EMTs took care of them. I saw that more than half a dozen of them were children, and they looked as dirty and undernourished as the adults. It was a horrible scene.

Odelia joined Chase, who stood discussing things with the same state trooper we'd seen earlier. It was clear this thing was big, as more cops arrived.

"Who can do such a thing?" Dooley asked as we approached the house.

"Humans," said Brutus.

"Greedy humans," I corrected him.

"You're right," he conceded. "Not all humans are the same."

"Odelia would never do something like this," said Dooley.

"No, you're right about that," Brutus admitted. "Odelia is a saint."

And he meant it, too.

We darted inside the house, making sure we didn't get in the way of the cops who were still coming and going. We passed what looked like barracks for the workers to sleep. Rickety tables and chairs. Bunk beds with ratty blankets and dirty old mattresses where they spent their nights.

Another large, ill-lit and ill-ventilated room held rows and rows of sewing machine stations, large ironing boards and piles and piles of material used to turn into the expensive, exclusive clothes sold under the Ziv Riding label. There was a pile of those labels, and I wondered who'd written the notes that had been smuggled out sewed inside those labels.

"This is way depressing," Dooley said.

"Yeah, even more depressing than Diego," Brutus chimed in.

We quickly took a peek in the lavatories—as dirty and unhygienic as any I'd ever seen—and the canteen where the workforce had taken their meals—and then I'd had enough. This much human misery I'd never seen before. Even cats were treated better in Hampton Cove.

"I hope they catch whoever is responsible for this and lock them up for a long stretch," I said as we stepped out and breathed in fresh air again.

"Or better yet, lock them up and throw away the key," said Brutus.

"Must be this Ziv Riding guy, right?" Dooley ventured a guess.

We returned to where Odelia and Chase stood discussing things and parked ourselves at their feet. I didn't want to be trampled on by the dozens of cops and other personnel that had by now descended on the site, and I didn't feel like walking all the way back to the center of town, so sticking close to Odelia was our best option. Sticking close to Odelia was always our best option, period.

"So what's going to happen now?" Odelia asked.

"Now we're going to talk to our NYPD colleagues and ask them to arrest Ziv Riding," Chase replied.

"Do you think he knew about this?"

"I can't see how he wouldn't. This is his collection being created here. How could he not know?"

"I don't know," she said, looking at the dozens of people still being led to the ambulances. "The people at the top don't always know what's going on at the bottom."

"Riding is a control freak. I'm sure there's no aspect of his business he's not fully aware of."

"Then I hope he goes to jail for this," she said resolutely.

"Hey, that's what I just said," I said.

"And I hope they lock him up and throw away the key," Chase grunted.

"And that's what I said!" Brutus cried.

Yep. Cats often turn into their humans. Or the other way around.

"So do you think we're getting meat tonight?" Dooley asked, already losing interest in the human drama in progress right in front of us.

"I hope so," said Brutus. "I haven't had a decent piece of meat in ages."

"And here we always thought you got raw meat every single day," I said.

"Yeah, I kinda lied about that," he admitted.

"But why?" Dooley asked.

He heaved an exasperated groan. "It's complicated."

"Explain it to me," said Dooley. "I'm smart. I'll understand."

Brutus gave him a dubious look.

"Explain it me, and I'll explain it to Dooley in two-syllable words," I said.

"Hey!" Dooley cried. "I'm right here!"

"When I saw how good you guys had it with the Pooles, I kinda got jealous," Brutus admitted. "So I decided to…"

"Make it look like you had it better than us?" I suggested.

He nodded, a little embarrassed. "Something like that. I just figured if you thought I ate raw meat every day, you wouldn't feel sorry for me."

"Feel sorry for you!" Dooley exclaimed. "Why would we feel sorry for you?!"

"Because you don't know how good you've got it!" he barked. "You just don't."

"Yes, we do," I said softly.

"Yes, we do," Dooley echoed happily. "And now you do, too, buddy."

"Thanks," Brutus said in a choky voice. "Thanks, you guys. And sorry that I was such a pest."

"That's all right. We haven't been very nice to you either," I said.

"Well, I deserved it."

"Yes, you did," Dooley said.

We all laughed, and for the first time I was starting to think that we might actually be friends one day. I wasn't saying we would, but there was definitely a chance.

CHAPTER 24

*U*ncle Alec had called to say he had big news. A breakthrough in the Niklaus Skad murder case. So Odelia and Chase had hurried over to the police station for an update. The state police were handling the sweatshop business, and would liaise with the NYPD to establish Ziv Riding's involvement—if any.

They arrived at the station house and walked right on through to Chief Alec's office. The big man was lounged in his chair, checking his computer screen. A first for the chief. He usually left all the computer business to younger, savvier officers or Chase.

He looked up when they entered, sporting the typical slightly confused and frustrated expression of a man not used to working on a PC.

"Hey, Uncle," Odelia said. "So what's this breakthrough you were talking about?"

"Well, looks like we finally cracked the case," he said, then pounded a few keys on his keyboard angrily and finally threw up his hands with an exasperated groan. "How you youngsters can figure out this crap is beyond me. How do I open Niklaus Skad's emails again? I know you showed me just yesterday, Chase, but I've gone and forgotten all about it."

Chase walked around the desk and took over the mouse and keyboard. "You just click here and type in your password and you're in," he explained.

Chief Alec gave Odelia a grimace. "It's all Chinese to me. I'm happy I can check my own emails. I don't need to check anyone else's."

"What did you want to check?" Chase asked, stepping back.

"Well, the coroner called about an hour ago. He said he's been all wrong about the time of death. Apparently it was a little tough to establish an exact time with the body being all burned up. But he did some more tests, and said time of death was an hour, hour-and-a-half earlier than he initially thought. Which means…" he said meaningfully, his eyes glittering.

"That we have to recheck all of the suspects' alibis," Odelia completed the sentence.

"Already done that," said the Chief, picking up a yellow legal pad. He held it up. "This beats any computer any day in my book."

"That's because you're old, Chief," Chase teased.

"Yeah, I'm old, and I'm not too proud to admit it!"

"So where does this leave us?" Odelia asked, already going over each suspect in her mind.

"Well, let's see what we've got," said the Chief, frowning at his notes, which looked pretty illegible to Odelia. "According to Abe, time of death was around eleven, and not after midnight. Brainard and Isabella were engaged with their Echo from nine until three o'clock at night."

"That was a marathon session," said Chase with a glint of amusement.

"You can say that again. Guess I'll have to read up on my Kama Sutra one of these days."

"Or get yourself an Echo," Odelia suggested.

"Never in my life," said the Chief adamantly. "So who else is on this list? Hendrik Serarols. He's in the clear, too. His interview at the other restaurant, which took place over a late dinner with the proprietor, lasted from eleven until well after midnight. And since he also had to get there and back, he's in the clear."

"Too bad," said Chase. "I liked him as a suspect."

"That leaves us with Cybil Truscott," the Chief continued. "Whose toy boy exploits started around ten, as evidenced by multiple witnesses."

"And Facebook videos," Odelia added.

"So that leaves her out as well."

"What about Stacie Roebuck?" Chase asked. "The bullied assistant?"

"Well, I talked to the guy in charge of security at the Hampton Springs Hotel. They have some complicated system installed, where they can check time stamps on the key cards. They were so kind to check the log for Room 327 and found that Miss Roebuck was in from nine until six o'clock in the morning, when she apparently went for a morning jog."

"She could have snuck out through the window and jumped to the balcony of the next room," Odelia said, remembering how Max, Dooley and Brutus said they'd gained access to Stacie's room.

Her uncle pointed a finger at her. "And that's why I had the neighbors checked. The family staying in 325 were in all night. Only left the room for dinner, and then retired for the night. Same story with the septuagenarian in 326. He went to bed at nine and got up at five to go for a walk."

"Very boring people," Chase muttered. "Who stays in all night?"

"Families and old folks," said Uncle Alec with a stern look at him. "They can't all be Cybil Truscotts or partying teenagers, Chase."

"Fair enough," he said, holding up his hands.

"Besides, I thought we already established that Stacie Roebuck doesn't have the kind of physical strength needed to carry out this murder?" Alec added.

"Just making sure we've covered all the bases," Chase said.

"Next—and now it gets interesting," said the Chief, "is Konrad Daines." He settled back, a smug expression on his face. "Mr. Daines was arrested for disorderly conduct and public intoxication when he crashed the Clintons' party."

"So? That gives him a rock-solid alibi," said Chase.

"Officers were called to the scene at two o'clock in the morning," the Chief added triumphantly. "We talked to the people he was partying with, and that particular party only started after midnight. So we have no idea what Mr. Daines was up to before that time. That wasn't a problem when we thought Niklaus had been killed after midnight, but now…"

"He just might have done it," Chase said.

"Exactly."

Odelia stared at her uncle. "So you think Konrad Daines is our guy?"

"I think Konrad Daines is our guy," the Chief confirmed. "And to that effect I've sent a couple of officers around to the hotel to pick him up." He checked his watch. "They should be back any minute now."

"We talked to Konrad," Chase reminded Alec. "I liked him as a suspect."

"Oh, and one other thing," said the Chief. "I remembered seeing an email Niklaus wrote to Konrad. That's why I was trying to access the emails." He turned the screen so Odelia could follow along. Her uncle quickly scrolled through the emails, then tapped the screen with his pudgy finger. "Here it is. I knew I'd seen it flash by."

"You have to click the mouse to open the email, Uncle," Odelia said. "Tapping it with your finger won't work."

"Unless he's got a touchscreen," Chase added.

"I know that!" the Chief cried. "I may not know a lot about computers, but I know how to use a mouse!" He clicked to open the email. "Listen to this," he said. "This is from the day before Niklaus died. 'I heard about *Chopped Liver* being, well, chopped. I'm so sorry about your loss, Konrad. Not! I told you *Kitchen Disasters* was the superior show and I was the superior chef and now I've gone and proved it. I hope this will show you that I'm the greatest celebrity chef in the world, and you'll always be a second-rate amateur. Take that, you whiny loser!'"

"That wasn't very nice," Chase said.

"No, that was outright mean," Odelia said, shocked.

"And I think it's motive," said the Chief. "Konrad got this email, spent the day chewing on it, and by the time evening rolled around, he'd gone and whipped himself up into a frenzy of rage and revenge. He knew Niklaus was in town, and most likely to be found at *Fry Me for an Oyster*, so he went there on the off chance he'd find him. They met—they fought—he killed him and then shoved him into the oven to get rid of the evidence. And *then* he went on his bender."

"Stacie said Niklaus never visited the restaurants he did," Odelia said. "Konrad would never have found him there."

"So he bumped into him somewhere else, and they went to the restaurant together. Or maybe he called him and they met out there."

It all sounded a little fuzzy to her. "Has Abe discovered the cause of death yet?"

"No, he hasn't. Most likely scenario is that Skad was

strangled. But since the soft tissue around the neck is gone, he won't be able to prove it."

"So now all you have to do is get a confession and it's case closed," said Chase.

"You also think Konrad is our guy?" Odelia asked.

"Why? Don't you?"

She shook her head slowly. "Something doesn't sit right with me."

"He's got motive!" cried her uncle. "He had opportunity. He's our guy!"

"Remember when we went to visit him, Chase?" she asked. "How he was certain we were there to talk about the drunk and disorderly thing?"

"So? He lied. He's a TV personality. I'm sure he knows a thing or two about acting."

"He didn't strike me as dishonest," she insisted. "He genuinely thought we were there to talk about Bill Clinton's party. He had no clue we were there to talk about the murder."

The two men shrugged. "I say we've got our guy," the Chief repeated.

It was definitely possible, of course. After all, being taunted in such a mean way could have made Konrad Daines snap, especially on the day his own show had been canceled and he was already feeling very low. Still, the impression she got from him wasn't that he was a killer.

Ten minutes later, the officers who'd gone to fetch Konrad finally arrived, the fallen celebrity chef in tow, and put him into the interrogation room. Chase and Odelia followed her uncle and watched through the one-way mirror as the latter entered the room and took a seat across from Konrad. The man looked much the worse for wear, as if being arrested was the final straw to his collapse.

"Mr. Daines," her uncle began. "It's come to my attention

that Niklaus Skad wrote you an email the day before he died."

Konrad stared at him. His bristly hair stood in all directions, and his skin had gone pale and blotchy. "An email?"

"Yes. Shall I read it to you? Jog your memory?" And as he did, Konrad's face grew paler still. He looked nothing like the famous TV chef he was.

"I remember," he said in a hoarse whisper. "Niklaus was an animal. I hated him so much—so very, very much."

"Is that why you killed him?"

Konrad stared at Chief Alec, his lips moving wordlessly.

The Chief slammed the table. "You hated him so much you killed him, isn't that right, Konrad?"

The chef started shaking. It was clear he was in the throes of a breakdown. "Yes," he finally whispered.

"Yes, what?"

"Yes, I wanted him dead. I wanted him dead so, so much. I wanted to kill him—cut him—skewer him—chop off his head —rip him to pieces!"

Spittle was flying from his lips now, his eyes wild and crazy.

"So you admit you killed him," her uncle said calmly.

"Yes! Yes, I killed Niklaus Skad!" Konrad suddenly cried, getting up from his chair. "I killed the greatest chef alive! Me, Konrad Daines! I destroyed the monster! I finished him off like the worm he was! I did it!"

"Settle down, Mr. Daines," said the Chief, looking a little worried.

"I think he's lost it," Odelia said.

"I think you're right," Chase agreed. "But he still confessed."

"I killed him! The monster is dead! The monster is dead!" Konrad screamed, pounding the walls of the room.

Uncle Alec darted a glimpse at the one-way mirror. He didn't look at ease.

"I think we better get a couple of officers in there," said Chase. "Before he attacks your uncle."

"The monster is dead! The monster is finally dead!"

The Chief hurried out of the room while three officers moved in to restrain Konrad. When he joined them, he was wiping perspiration from his brow. "Phew. The guy just went nuts on me."

"At least you got your confession," Odelia said.

They both watched Konrad pick up a chair and smash it on the table. "Yeah, at least we got his confession," Uncle Alec said, scratching his head.

"The monster is dead! I killed him! I killed him dead! Me! I won!"

Somehow, there was something wrong with this picture, Odelia thought. Whatever Konrad said, she couldn't help feeling the real killer was still out there.

CHAPTER 25

Odelia had dropped the three of us off at the police station, where she had some urgent business to take care of. She said there had been some kind of breakthrough in the case of the celebrity chef, so that was great. Most likely Chief Alec had caught the killer and now Hampton Cove would return to its usual peaceful state. It let us off the hook, as we no longer had to root around to catch the killer. Not that I minded. For some reason sleuthing came naturally to me. Probably because I'm a naturally curious cat. It's just the way I'm wired, I guess.

We were traipsing along Main Street when we saw Gran ducking into some alley with that ancient boyfriend of hers. Oh, God. Not again.

"Wasn't that your human?" Brutus asked.

Dooley looked up, completely oblivious as usual. "Huh?"

"Gran just went into that alley with Leo," I said.

"She did? Maybe we should see what she's up to?" Dooley suggested.

"Why would we want to see what she's up to?" I asked.

"Yeah, it's really none of our business," Brutus said, not sounding too keen.

"She's my human, you guys!" Dooley cried. "I have a responsibility!"

"I think it's the other way around, Dooley," I said. "She has a responsibility towards you, not you towards her."

"It goes both ways," he said stubbornly. "She looks after me, so I need to look after her. What if this guy Leo is up to no good? What then? And I just sat here while she was being assaulted or something!"

"She's not being assaulted," I said. "It's just that she can't take Leo home because nobody approves of him, so they've gone and taken their affair to the streets."

"Weird," said Brutus.

"What's weird?" I asked.

"I always thought human adults could do whatever they wanted. That it was just teenagers and kids that had to sneak around their parents' backs."

"Once you reach a certain age you revert back to the same state of having to sneak around," I said. "Only now you sneak around your kids' backs."

"I still think it's weird," Brutus said with a shrug.

Well, it was kinda weird, of course. Once upon a time Marge had probably snuck around with Tex, canoodling in backseats of cars or bushes near the beach, and now it was Gran's turn to do the same to her daughter. It was probably the circle of life or something. Like *The Lion King*.

"The more I learn about humans the more I think they're way weird," Brutus insisted.

"Better not to think about it too much," Dooley said.

Of course, Dooley never thought about anything too much, so for him that came naturally.

We'd reached the alley, and darted a peek around the corner, fully expecting to see stuff that would hurt our eyes.

Instead, I saw something that horrified me to my core. There was Diego, and there was a cat, but that cat wasn't Harriet!

"Um, am I seeing this right?" asked Brutus. "Is Diego putting the moves on that feline over there?"

"You are seeing this right!" I said.

We all stared. Diego was doing stuff to that feline I'd never seen before, unless in those nature documentaries on the *Discovery Channel*. I mean, I have been with a female before, of course, but I'd never done… that!

"What are they doing?" Dooley asked.

"Something that's not suitable for young viewers," Brutus growled.

"I'm not a young viewer," said Dooley.

"Well, you're not an old viewer either," Brutus said. He let out a long sigh of relief. "You know what this means, right?"

"That Diego is the hottest stud ever to walk these streets?" I asked.

"No! That Diego is cheating on Harriet."

"Oh. Right," I said. I was so fascinated by the moves Diego was demonstrating that the thought of Harriet hadn't even occurred to me.

Dooley twisted his head to try and get the upside-down view. "No, but what *are* they doing?" he asked.

"If I tell Harriet about this, she'll break up with Diego in a heartbeat!" Brutus said.

"She won't believe you," I said automatically. I was also twisting my head one-hundred-and-eighty degrees. This stuff was fascinating. I was learning things I'd never seen before, not even on the *Discovery Channel*.

"She'll have to believe me!" Brutus exclaimed. "You guys are going to back me up on this, right? You're my witnesses."

"Sure. But she won't believe us either," I said.

"But why? You're her friends!"

"Trust me, Brutus. When it comes to matters of the heart,

a female feline only believes what she wants to believe. And if she wants to believe Diego is God's gift to cats, nothing we say will convince her otherwise."

"We need proof!" Brutus said, searching around. "We need Odelia with her phone. She needs to film this! She needs to get this on video and show Harriet!"

"Even so. Harriet is not going to believe it unless she sees it with her own eyes," I said. "Trust me on this, Brutus. That's just the way it is."

"Oh, God!" he cried. "This is just one big nightmare, isn't it?"

"Do you think it hurts?" Dooley asked, now lying on his back.

"I don't think so," I said.

"But they're panting. And look at her. She looks like she's in pain!"

"That's not an expression of pain, Dooley," I said. "That's... rapture."

"Rapture? What's rapture?"

"Nothing you'll ever experience," I promised him.

"But why?!"

"Just think about the juiciest chicken wing God ever created."

He frowned, thinking hard. "Uh-huh."

"Now multiply that sensation by about a million."

"Oh, my," he said, eyes widening.

"Exactly."

"Look, I'm going to get Odelia. She needs to see this," Brutus said, sounding very agitated. "She'll back me up. If she says Diego was doing the horizontal mambo with some other chick, Harriet has got to believe her."

"What's the horizontal mambo?" Dooley asked.

"Oh, Dooley," I said with a sigh.

Brutus went off on his fool's errand, and I stared after

him for a moment. And that's when I saw it. A Tesla, driving along Main Street. A very black Tesla.

"Dooley!" I said.

"Huh?"

"It's the Tesla!"

He glanced the way I was looking. "Nice wheels."

"It's the car that was parked behind the restaurant that night! It's got to be!"

And before he could respond, I broke into a run, in hot pursuit of the Tesla. I needed to get a glimpse at the license plate. I needed to figure out who that car belonged to. And as I came racing out of the alley, I saw that the car stopped right in front of a boutique store, halfway down the street. Panting, I came running up, and I watched as a tall Asian man stepped from the car and disappeared into the store. He was elegantly dressed in a kind of cape draped across his shoulders, shiny slicked-back black hair and snazzy sunglasses. I glanced at the license plate. It said Z1VR1D1N. I stared. Huh? Then I got it. ZIV RIDING!

$\mathcal{K}$onrad Daines had been charged with the murder of his celebrity chef rival and arrested. A lawyer was on his way over, though it was obvious there wasn't a lot he'd be able to do for his client. Konrad had confessed. Case closed.

And Odelia was just about to go to the Gazette to write up the shocking story of the two rival TV stars, when Brutus came barging into the police station, meowing up a storm.

"You have to come with me, Odelia," he pleaded.

She quickly glanced around, but Dolores had gone on a bathroom break, and Chase was still in the Chief's office, discussing the denouement of the case. She crouched down. "What happened? Are you hurt?"

"Nobody's hurt! It's Diego!" Brutus said between two pants. He looked as if he'd been running, his heart beating a mile a minute.

"Diego? What about Diego?"

"He's with another cat! You have to come along as my witness."

"He's with a cat? You mean, in the biblical sense?"

He stared at her blankly. "I don't know what that means."

"I mean, are they... smooching?"

He gave a disgusted snort. "Not just smooching. They're having sex!"

She laughed, tickling Brutus behind his ears. "Oh, my. And we can't have that, right?"

"No, we can't! I mean, of course we *can*, but Harriet... I mean..."

"I think I understand. You want me to tell Harriet that Diego is with some other cat, being unfaithful to her, so you and Harriet can get back together."

"That's it! You're so smart!"

She sighed, getting up. "I can't do that, Brutus. I can't be a snitch on my own cats. If you feel Diego isn't doing right by Harriet, you have to tell her, but I'm not going to sneak around and spy on him so I can tell on him to Harriet."

"But why?! He shouldn't be doing that!"

"That's not for me to judge, Brutus. And, honestly, I think you should just let it go. I'm sure Harriet will find out soon enough what kind of cat Diego is. And she doesn't need you to tell her."

"But I... love her!"

"Then you'll just have to trust her to do the right thing."

"But how is she going to know about Diego if I don't tell her?"

"She'll know," she said with a smile. "But if you go and snitch on Diego, she'll lose all respect for Diego, and she'll lose all respect for you, too."

Brutus groaned in agony. "Why is everything always so complicated?!"

"I'm glad it's not just us humans that make things complicated," she said.

Just then, Max came slamming into the police station. "Odelia! You have to see this!"

She held up her hand. "Brutus already told me all about Diego, Max. And I told him I wouldn't turn snitch on my own cats."

"Who cares about Diego?!" Max cried. "It's the Tesla! I saw the Tesla!"

Her curiosity piqued, she bent down again. "The black Tesla?"

He nodded furiously. "It belongs to Ziv Riding. He's got one of those vanity plates, that's how I found out. He went into one of the boutiques on Main Street."

Now this was definitely interesting. "I think I better go and get Chase," she said, and gave Max a pat on the head. "Well done, buddy. Great sleuthing."

"Thanks," he said, then caught Brutus's scowl. "What?"

"Nothing," said Brutus. "Just that I thought you'd back me up on the Diego thing."

Max rolled his eyes. "Oh, God. Enough with the Diego thing already."

She left the two cats and went in search of Chase. They needed to check up on this Tesla sighting. She hadn't told Chase cats had seen the black Tesla parked behind *Fry Me for an Oyster*, and neither would she tell Riding. It was enough that an anonymous witness had seen the car. She needn't involve Max.

She stuck her head into her uncle's office. "The black Tesla has been sighted. And guess what? It belongs to Ziv Riding."

"Sweatshop Ziv Riding?" Chase asked.

"Yep. One and the same."

"Well, go on, then," said the Chief. "Go ask him what he was doing here the night of the murder."

They didn't need her uncle's encouragement. She and Chase were hotfooting it out of the police station and hurrying along the street before Chief Alec had managed to get up from his seat.

"So who saw the car?" Chase asked.

"I did, actually," she said after a moment's pause.

"I thought you said the Tesla had been sighted?"

"Yeah, by me. It was sighted by me."

He gave her a curious look. "Why didn't you just say that?"

She flapped her hands a bit. "I was so excited I couldn't think straight!"

"Right," he said, and she had the impression he didn't believe one word she said. But she couldn't worry about that now. They needed to figure out what the fashion designer had been doing that night at the restaurant.

"Are you sure it's the same car that was parked in the alley that night?"

"Not a hundred percent sure, no," she admitted.

"I mean, there must be hundreds of Teslas, thousands, even. And a lot of them are black."

"I guess so," she said.

"So what makes you think it was Riding's car?"

She paused for a moment. "Actually…"

He gave her a wry look and halted, right in front of the General Store. "What's going on, Odelia? Why are you going about half-cocked?"

She flapped her arms again, looking more like a chicken than a reporter. "I have a hunch, all right?"

"A hunch," he said skeptically. He'd crossed his arms over his chest and stood regarding her with his head to one side, as if wondering what to do with her.

"A hunch! I have a hunch that this Tesla is that Tesla!"

"You never told me who the witness was that saw the Tesla that night."

"I—I can't. I—I promised I wouldn't reveal her name."

"If you'll just let me talk to her I might get a confirmation on the license plate."

She shook her head decidedly. "She didn't see the license plate."

"Are you sure?"

"Positive." She wondered what would happen if she told Chase Max had heard it from Montserrat, the stray Erin Coka had taken under her wing, who'd heard it from some other stray. He'd probably have her 5150ed.

"So let me get this straight," he said. "Someone—who doesn't want to be named—told you she saw a black Tesla parked outside the restaurant the night Niklaus Skad was killed. No license plate. Now you see another black Tesla, driven by Ziv Riding, parked along the street, and you want to talk to the man, why, exactly?"

"Don't you think it's too much of a coincidence? Ziv Riding has this sweatshop in town, and his car was seen at a murder scene?"

"We don't even know if Riding and Skad knew each other. And may I remind you that we caught Skad's killer? He's in custody right now. The case is closed, Odelia."

"But what about the sweatshop thing?"

"Not our concern! We're not handling that investigation and we're not going to get involved, either."

She shook her head, stubbornly. "I still feel—"

"It's not about what you 'feel,'" he said. "It's about the facts." He raked his fingers through his mane. "Oh, God. And I almost went along with this nonsense. Me and your uncle." He held up his hands. "Look, you're on your own with this. Please don't involve me. And may I add that I have a strong suspicion you're not telling me everything you know?"

They stared at each other, and then she said. "I know Riding's Tesla was parked at the restaurant. And I'm going to find out what's going on. With or without you."

"Well, it's going to be without me, honey," he said, stepping back. "Like I said, you're on your own from here on out."

And without another word, he turned around and started walking back to the police station.

Nice, she thought. Nicely played, Odelia. So now what?

CHAPTER 27

*B*rutus and I walked out of the police station and back to the alley, where presumably Dooley still sat watching—and having his youthful innocence thoroughly screwed up.

"Odelia should have backed us up," Brutus said. "She should have had our backs."

"Odelia has our backs," I said. "All of our backs, Diego included."

"But how is that even possible?! Diego isn't even part of our family."

"He is to her. The moment that cat set foot inside her home, he became family."

"It's just not fair."

"You don't get it, do you? Odelia doesn't play favorites. She doesn't love one of us more than the others. And she's right about Harriet. She's smarter than you give her credit for. Have you ever considered Harriet has Diego's number?"

"She can't have his number. She doesn't even know he's out here."

"Let's just wait and see," I said. "First things first, though.

We have to get Dooley out of there. Diego is a bad influence on him."

We arrived at the alley. To my surprise there was no trace of Dooley.

"Where did he go?" I muttered, looking around.

"And where did Diego go?" asked Brutus. There were dumpsters parked along the alley, butting up to the bricked-up back walls of the stores that lined the parallel street. We headed deeper into the alley, half expecting to find Gran and Leo cavorting around somewhere. What we found were Dooley and Diego, however, seated behind a dumpster and deep in conversation.

"So that's the secret, dude," Diego was saying. "You just snag 'em, bag 'em and then throw 'em back."

"But won't they resent you for it?" Dooley asked.

"What do you care? There's plenty of cats in the sea. When you're finished with one, you just start tagging another one."

Dooley laughed. "Tag 'em, snag 'em and bag 'em. That rhymes!"

"It sure does," said Diego with a smirk. "I'm glad you're catching on, dude."

"Let me just stop you right there," I said, stepping from behind the dumpster.

"Max!" Dooley cried. "Diego's been teaching me all about his technique for bagging queens! Isn't that great?!"

I winced. "Not so great. Queens aren't a commodity to be tagged, snagged and bagged, Dooley. They're our fellow creatures and they deserve our respect."

"What a load of nonsense," said Diego. "Don't listen to him, Dooley. You just do what I taught you, and you'll have the females eating out of the palm of your paw for the rest of your life. Just like they do with me. They'll just swoon!"

"Well, I certainly would like females to swoon," Dooley said.

"Just think about Harriet," I said. "And how Diego has been treating her."

"Hey, I treated Harriet just fine," said Diego. He grinned. "Just ask her. She said she's never been with a cat that made her feel the way I did."

"That's a lie!" Brutus yelled.

Diego held up his paw. "Straight from the cat's mouth, brother."

"Females are not chattel, Dooley," I said sternly. "You need to treat them with respect, just like you do with everyone."

"Don't listen to that wuss," said Diego. "He doesn't know what he's talking about."

"Hey, who are you calling a wuss?" Brutus snarled, stepping to my defense.

"You! All of you! You're just a bunch of pussies."

Well, he was right about that, of course. We were pussies.

"You take that back!" Brutus yelled.

Diego displayed a wide grin and lifted his paw, displaying sharp claws. "And what if I don't?"

"Don't be like that, you guys," said Dooley. "Diego is our friend. He can teach us stuff. Lots of interesting stuff."

"Whatever Diego told you, you better forget, Dooley," I said. "All of it."

Diego apparently had had enough. He suddenly stepped up and hit me, hard, across the nose. "Ouch!" I cried as blood trickled down my snout.

"See?!" Diego cried. "Your friend is just a dumb scaredy-cat, Dooley. Can't even defend himself!"

Dooley sat staring at me. "Max? Is he right? Are you a scaredy-cat?"

I would have told him I was a lover, not a fighter, but that just didn't seem right under the circumstances. Instead, I glowered at Diego. Truth was, I'm not much of a brawler. I like to think I'm above physical violence. And then there was the fact that Diego looked a lot fitter and stronger than me, and I had the sneaking suspicion he was going to beat me in a fair fight.

"Don't you go hitting my friend, you sneaky snake in the grass," Brutus growled.

Diego had gone through quite the transformation. His tail was fluffed up and he was making low growling sounds at the back of his throat. His claws were out and his head was down, snarling and hissing at Brutus. Yep. He was ready to fight.

Brutus, seeing this, seemed taken aback. "Go on," I said. "You can beat him!"

But Brutus didn't seem entirely sure. "I don't know, Max," he said. "He looks really mean."

And then suddenly, out of nowhere, Diego lashed out, slashing Brutus across the face with his claws. Brutus said, "Eek!" and jumped back just in time to avoid the razor-sharp claws of his opponent, then sat there, his tail between his legs.

Diego huffed out a booming laugh. "See, Dooley? Your friends are just a couple of pussies!" He draped a paw around Dooley's shoulder. "You stick with me from now on, buddy. I'll teach you everything I know."

"Dooley!" I cried. "Don't go with him!"

Dooley glanced back. He seemed confused and conflicted.

All of a sudden there was a loud CLUNK right next to us. I jerked my head up, and saw that a cat had landed on the dumpster. She was a feral cat, her fur all mangled and matted and missing in parts. She looked like she'd been in more fights than the members of *Fight Club*, and had a scar that ran through one of her eyes. She looked like a monster. I recognized her instantly.

"Clarice!" I cried.

"Oh, no, not Clarice," Brutus said with a whimper, and Dooley, too, didn't look happy to see her. He clasped a hand to his nose, which tended to get slashed every time we got involved with the wild cat.

"Who the hell are you?" Diego asked, giving her the evil eye.

"I am your worst nightmare," she hissed, slowly moving along the top of the dumpster, her claws scratching the metal. "I am the one female that will never be seduced by your clever lines, your smooth tongue or your treacherous lies."

"You're not a female," Diego said with a careless laugh. "I don't know what you are, but you're definitely not on my list. Just look at her, Dooley. Ha ha! Look at that mongrel, dude!"

But Dooley wasn't laughing, and neither was the rest of us.

"Better hold your tongue, Diego," she hissed, running a claw along the edge of the dumpster. "Or I just might cut it out!"

"What an idiot!" Diego laughed. "And ugly as the night, too!"

"Max, Brutus and Dooley are my friends," Clarice declared, quite surprisingly. "You mess with my friends, you mess with me!"

"Well, come on then," said Diego. "If you want to rumble, let's rumble!"

Clarice displayed a sly smile. "Oh, you're asking for it? Well, fine."

And with these words, she jumped from the dumpster, right on top of Diego's head. For the next few seconds, there was a blur of activity as the two cats fought. There was a lot of hissing, a lot of snarling, and even more vicious clawing

170

going on. Fur was flying as claws were scratching and hitting their mark.

Then, as suddenly as it had all started, it was over. There was a loud squeak of pain, and a whirr of orange as Diego raced off, his tail between his legs, missing a good chunk of fur and leaving a trail of blood as he streaked off, caterwauling all the while.

Clarice, who seemed unharmed, sat casually licking the blood from her claws. "That should teach that misguided Romeo a lesson he'll never forget."

"Clarice, you're my hero!" suddenly a voice rang out behind us.

We all looked around, and saw that we'd been joined by Harriet.

She sat looking at the spot of orange in the distance that was Diego.

"How long have you been sitting there?" I asked.

"Long enough to hear Diego's mean-spirited and outright horrible advice," she said softly. "And even long enough to see him with that other cat." She gestured up. "I was actually on the roof. I'd followed him here when he went out. Said he was going to get a breath of fresh air." She shook her head. "I knew he was up to no good. A player like him?"

Clarice stared at the spot of orange that grew smaller and smaller. "I don't think he'll be back, honey. I hope you don't mind."

"No, I don't," she said. "In fact I should have been the one to teach him a lesson." She nodded at the feral cat. "Thank you, Clarice."

Clarice shrugged. "Eh. Just a little community service. I had my eye on that player for a while. Nasty little devil. I enjoyed it, actually. It's not every day that I can take out the good old claws and get a little practice in."

"I'm so sorry, Brutus," Harriet said. "I know I hurt you terribly."

"Oh, sweetie pie," Brutus muttered brokenly. "Sugar plum."

"Oh, hugsy wugsy," Harriet sighed. "My huggy boo. Forgive me?"

"Of course, sweet cheeks. In a heartbeat."

"Oh, cuddle cakes."

The big reunion scene was both endearing and massively annoying, and I had to turn away when Harriet and Brutus started sniffing each other's butts, just like old times.

"Ugh," Clarice said. "I'm out of here. This is too much for me."

This from the cat that took on bullies twice her size and fed on rats that would have scared the average human.

"Bye, Clarice," Dooley said.

"See ya next time," Clarice said, padding off. "Stay out of trouble, you two."

We looked on as she gracefully jumped up on a dumpster, then onto a ledge, and then made her way to the roof of the nearest store.

Dooley let out a long sigh of admiration. "What a cat," he said.

"Yeah, what a cat," I agreed heartily.

Dooley turned to me. "I'm sorry I doubted you, Max."

"That's all right."

"No, you were right. Diego was a bad influence. It's just that... he sounded so convincing."

"That's the power of the dark side for you, Dooley," I said.

"Oh, is that what that was?" he asked, eyes wide. "It's so powerful!"

"Yeah, good thing Clarice showed up and brought you back to the light."

"Right," he said. "So Clarice is like Princess Leia, huh?"

"Um... something like that, I guess."

We looked at Harriet and Brutus, in the midst of their make-up scene, and both turned away and started making our way out of the alley.

"I think I'm way too young for all that dating stuff, Max."

"I think you're right, Dooley."

"It just looks very complicated."

"Uh-huh."

"I don't like complicated, Max."

"Me neither, Dooley. Me neither."

CHAPTER 28

Odelia stubbornly walked on. If Chase didn't want to confront Ziv Riding about his nocturnal visit to Hampton Cove, she was. She stalked over in the direction of the boutique where Max said he'd seen the Tesla parked, and saw Riding leaving the store and returning to his vehicle.

She hurried over, wanting to catch him before he skedaddled. The store was Riding's, and exclusively carried the Ziv Riding brand.

"Mr. Riding!" she yelled. "Mr. Riding! A word, sir!"

Riding turned around, his hand on the door of his car. He was a handsome man with smooth, even features and remarkable black eyes. A smile spread on his face when he saw her coming. "Of course I'll do a selfie, darling. But only one. And only from the right. That's my best side."

"My name is Odelia Poole, and I'm a reporter for the Hampton Cove Gazette and a civilian consultant with the Hampton Cove Police Department."

His smile faltered. "No selfie?"

"No," she said decidedly. "No selfie. Someone saw your

car parked behind *Fry Me for an Oyster* a couple of nights ago."

Now his smile was completely wiped away. "No comment, Miss…"

"Poole. Odelia Poole."

He opened his car door and made to get in. "Bye, Miss Poole."

"It was the same night Niklaus Skad was murdered, Mr. Riding. Would you care to comment?"

"No, I would rather not," he said as he slid into his seat. He tried to close the door, but Odelia held onto it. "What was your involvement with Niklaus Skad, Mr. Riding?"

"No involvement. I liked his cooking show, though. Now could you please let go of my door, Miss Poole? It's my door and I need it."

"What about the sweatshop you built in town? What was your involvement with that?"

"I don't know about any sweatshop. My clothes are all made in Asia. Now please if you could just…"

"Your clothes were made by Asian workers you illegally brought into this country and then set to work in appalling conditions."

"Thank you for your interest," he said. "Please schedule an interview with my publicist. I'm always happy to talk to the members of the press."

With a press of his finger, he started the car and drove off, closing the door as he moved away. It was amazing, Odelia thought. The car hardly made any noise. It just… glided away ever so gracefully. Then she groaned in dismay. The guy was as slippery as they came. And she had nothing on him. Nothing at all.

She mounted the sidewalk and staggered off, feeling utterly dejected. Chase thought she was a flake and that she was hiding something. She'd just angered a fashion designer who probably had nothing to do with this whole Niklaus Skad thing. And she had to sort out the mess her cats had made. This whole Diego versus Brutus thing was getting out of hand.

She set foot for the alley Brutus had been talking about. Maybe she should sort this out once and for all. It wasn't as if she had anything better to do. Like her uncle said, they caught the killer. He confessed. The rest was conjecture.

The first thing she saw when she entered the alley was Max and Dooley sauntering towards her. "Hey, Odelia," said Max. "How did it go with Ziv Riding?"

"It didn't. Though he drives a really cool car. How did things go with Diego?" Dooley jerked his thumb in the direction of the alley, and she saw Brutus and Harriet, smooching up a storm. "I take it things worked themselves out?"

"They certainly did," Max said. "With a little help from Clarice."

"Right," she said.

"Hey. Isn't that Grandma?" asked Max.

She looked in the direction indicated, and saw that it was indeed her grandmother, and she was looking just as dejected as she was feeling. She was shuffling along on the other side of the street. So she quickly crossed and joined her. "Gran? What's wrong?"

Gran looked up, her wrinkly face drawn. "Oh, I won't tell you."

"You won't tell me what?"

"You'll just laugh at me."

"I promise I won't laugh at you."

"It's Leo. He left me."

"He left you?"

"Yeah, for a younger woman. Can you believe it? We were making out in the park when some hot young dame sat down next to us. Leo's eyes wandered, the hot chick giggled, and then his hands wandered and next thing I knew he was making out with her instead of me! I just left."

"Some hot young chick made out with Leo? How old was this chick?"

"You know her. Frankie Canolli's grandmother Jackie."

"Jackie Canolli? But she's like a hundred!"

Gran gave her a hard stare. "She's younger than me!"

"Not by much." Odelia had been in school with Frankie. They were the same age.

"Didn't you tell her off? Or Leo?"

Gran shrugged her bony shoulders. "Ah. No use talking to Leo. We were never much for talking anyway. Ours was more a physical bond."

"I'll say," she muttered.

"And I'm not speaking to Jackie. Haven't said a word to her since she took my roast beef recipe and passed it off at the pinochle club as her own."

She placed an arm around her grandmother's shoulders. "I'm sorry. I didn't like Leo, but that's just because I didn't think he deserved you."

"I know he didn't deserve me, but at my age you can't afford to be choosy, honey."

They walked in silence for a while. "Chase is mad with me," she finally said.

"Oh? And why is that?"

"He thinks I'm hiding something from him."

"About the cats, huh?"

"Yeah. He knows something is going on but he can't figure out what it is and now he's mad I'm not telling him."

"So tell him."

She looked at her grandmother. "What?"

"Just tell him. See how he reacts. If he's fine with it, he's a keeper. If not..." She held up her hand. "Well, then at least you know he doesn't deserve you."

She gave her grandmother a hug. "Thanks, Gran. I won't tell him but still, thanks."

"If you're not going to tell him, and he's going to stay mad at you, can I have a shot at him?"

"Gran!"

"Just asking."

CHAPTER 29

*C*hase had placed his long legs on Chief Alec's desk, while the chief had done the same on his side. They sat staring out the window. Chase still couldn't get over the fact that Odelia would stubbornly insist they needed to go after this Ziv Riding character. The only thing the guy had done wrong—apart from running a sweatshop in this town—was drive the wrong car.

"I mean, you see that, right?" he asked for the umpteenth time. "It's a Tesla! Everybody drives a Tesla these days. A buddy of mine is visiting Belgium and he said it's full of Teslas over there. Frickin' Belgium, for crying out loud!"

"Is Belgium even a country? I thought it was a city."

"Pretty sure it's a country, Chief. Beer, chocolate and waffles?"

"Oh, right."

He lapsed into silence again. "And what about this cat business? There's something going on with those cats of hers. Like she's got some kind of intuition when it comes to Max. Is that even possible? Or normal?"

"Why not? It's called women's intuition, Chase. And Odelia loves her cats."

"But cats are just a bunch of dumb animals. They can't figure out that there's a sweatshop in town. Or that there's a black Tesla parked outside a restaurant. She's hiding something, Chief. She's got some secret informant and she won't reveal her name. Yeah, it's a she. She admitted that much."

"Odelia is a reporter, Chase. Working with informants is what she does. And you know how a reporter feels about protecting a source. It's important."

"I know that. I just…" He gave an annoyed grunt.

"You just hoped she would tell you all her secrets," the Chief said with a grin.

"Well, yeah. I mean, why wouldn't she? We work well together. She knows she can trust me. I won't reveal her sources to anyone."

"Just give her time, Chase. And don't push her. The more you push her to give up her secrets the more she's going to clamp up."

"So what you're saying is I should just let her harass this guy Ziv Riding?"

"He's no boy scout. He did organize a sweatshop."

"That doesn't make him a killer."

"No, it does not. It does make him a very bad man. Though it looks like he'll walk away from this mess. Guy lawyered up big time."

"Sure he did. He'll pay a big-ass fine and he'll go on making millions."

"Oh, before I forget, the NYPD guy I talked to said they found a link between Niklaus Skad and Riding. Wanna hear about it?"

He jerked up, almost dropping out of his chair. "What?"

"Yeah. Funny thing is, I found the same email in Skad's account."

"And you're only telling me this now?! Show me!"

"Hold your horses, cowboy. Now where is this darn thing…" He messed around on his computer, cursed a lot, and finally found it. "Here you go," he said, swiveling the screen and stabbing at it with his finger. "Read it and weep."

Chase scanned the email, then his eyes landed on the crucial paragraph. "I know about your dirty little secret and I'm not going to keep quiet unless you double your investment," he read with rising surprise. "This is non-negotiable, Riding. You better do as I say or else." Say what?

"Huh? Pretty explosive stuff."

"Jeez…" he said, absolutely dumbfounded. "Oh, my God…"

"What?" Chief Alec asked with a chuckle. "Just proves these celebrities are all in bed together. All one big happy family, huh?"

His brain worked feverishly. "So Riding was an investor in Skad's business. And somehow Skad had found out about the sweatshop and was threatening to expose it unless Riding doubled his investment."

"Do you think that's what he meant with 'dirty little secret?'"

"What else could it be?"

They stared at one another. "We have our killer, Chase. He confessed."

"What if Konrad isn't the killer? What if Riding's car really was parked outside the restaurant that night and he's the killer? Wanting to shut Skad up before he blew the lid on this whole sweatshop affair?"

Chief Alec shook his head. "I've got a confession."

"That wasn't a confession, Alec. That was a nervous breakdown. The guy didn't know what he was saying. He would have confessed to killing Kennedy or being Jack the Ripper."

The Chief thought about this as he picked up something from his desk. It was a fortune cookie. He absentmindedly toyed with it, then crumbled it under his fingers, took out the little piece of paper and popped the cookie into his mouth, munching down.

Chase stared at him. "What's that?"

"Huh? Oh, something the guys picked up at the sweat-shop. They had bags and bags of the stuff." He lobbed one at Chase and he deftly caught it. He studied the fortune cookie and something clicked inside his mind. There was a nicely designed logo printed on the cookie. A Z and an R. Ziv Riding. Probably PR swag. "Alec?"

"Mh?"

"Remember how the coroner found a fortune cookie in Niklaus Skad's stomach?"

The Chief stopped munching, and then his eyes went wide. "Oh, no."

"Oh, yes."

Odelia's uncle drew his hands through his few remaining wisps of hair. "Oh, Jesus. I locked up the wrong guy, didn't I?"

"And Odelia was right about Riding," said Chase, nodding.

"I should have known," said the Chief with a groan. "That damn niece of mine is always right!"

CHAPTER 30

*W*e were finally on our way home. This whole business with Diego had brought home to me the fact that I needed a break. I'd been up all day, and I needed to lie down and get some shut-eye. And we were just passing by the General Store when Kingman called out, "Max! Hey, Max!"

"Ignore him," I told Dooley. "I just want to go home and sleep."

"Max! Dooley!"

"I can't ignore him, Max," Dooley said. "He might have something important to say."

"He always has something important to say, but I need to get some sleep."

"Max! Dooley! Yoo-hoo! Over here!"

"Just ignore him," I said through gritted teeth.

But Dooley had already veered off course. I followed him with a tired moan.

"Max!" Kingman said. "Meet Norma."

I stared at the small white cat splayed out next to Kingman. The name didn't ring a bell. "Hi, Norma," I said out of sheer politeness.

"She's the cat I told you about," Kingman continued cheerfully. "About the sweatshop? I heard they closed down that operation. Can you believe it? A sweatshop? In our town? What is this, the nineteenth century or something?"

I studied Norma with more interest this time. "So you were out at the sweatshop, huh?"

"I was," said the cat in a melodious voice.

"That was really brave of you," said Dooley.

"Hardly," said Norma. "Humans never take any notice of cats. I could come and go as I pleased, even slip past the guards and walk right into that place."

"So do you think this guy Ziv Riding was involved?" I asked.

"Oh, definitely," said Norma. "He came out there at least once a month, to check up on production, and do some spot checks for quality control. I'd say he knew exactly what was going on out there."

Now this was news. Kingman grinned excitedly. "I told you she's the real deal, didn't I, Max? Huh? You owe me, right? Big time. Am I right or am I right?"

"You're right," I said reluctantly. Owing Kingman wasn't much fun. I needed to bring him a piece of gossip at least equal in size to the Ziv Riding sweatshop story, which was going to prove hard. Then suddenly I got an idea.

"Was Riding out there the night Niklaus Skad was killed?"

Norma displayed a hint of a smile. "If I tell you, what's in it for me?"

Let me tell you, all cats are hustlers. There are no exceptions.

"What do you want?" I asked.

"I heard you can talk to your human, is that true?"

"Yeah, it's true," I said with a dark look at Kingman, who shrugged.

"So tell her to bring me chocolate. And not the cheap kind Kingman's human carries. I want Swiss chocolate. The really expensive stuff."

"I'll get you your chocolate," I told her. "But chocolate isn't good for you."

"Let me worry about that."

"So? About Riding?"

"He was in town. He drove up to the farm in his black Tesla around ten o'clock. Wanted to make sure everything was running smoothly. I heard him talking to the guards. He said he had an appointment in town. Said he needed to get rid of a pesky problem and that he'd never been there."

"Get rid of a pesky problem. Were those his actual words?" I asked.

She gave me a cool, lingering look from beneath her long lashes. "I never lie, Max. If you'd bother to get to know me you'd realize that."

I gulped a little, and backed away slowly. The recent episode with Harriet and Diego was still fresh in my mind. I did not need female felines in my life right now. "Thanks, Norma," I said. "Much appreciated."

"Thanks, Norma!" said Dooley. "And we'd love to get to know you, wouldn't we, Max?"

She gave Dooley an appraising look, then said, "No, thank you. I don't date babies."

"Oh, burn!" Kingman shouted as Dooley and I walked away. "You owe me, Max!"

"And don't forget about the chocolate!" Norma added. "Swiss chocolate, Max! No cheap junk, you hear?!"

I held up my paw to show her I'd heard her loud and clear.

"What did she mean when she said she doesn't date

babies?" Dooley asked. "I'm not a baby. I'm just as old as you, Max. Should I have told her?"

"I thought you said you didn't need the complications of a relationship?"

Dooley glanced over his shoulder. "Yeah, but she looks really nice. I guess I could make an exception for her."

"Oh, Dooley," I said.

CHAPTER 31

Odelia was on her way to the Gazette when a squad car waylaid her. The car jumped the curb and she bumped into the hood. What the… She was even more surprised when Chase called out from inside the car, "Get in! You were right!"

"Of course I was right," she said as she got in. She slammed the door shut. "What was I right about, exactly?"

He gave her his best grin. "I owe you an apology, Odelia. First of all, you don't have to feel obligated to reveal your sources to me. You're a reporter. Your sources are sacred. I get that. Secondly, you were right about Riding. He and Skad were connected. Riding invested in Skad's business, and threatened to reveal the sweatshop business if Riding didn't increase his investment."

"I knew it!" she said, pounding the dashboard with her fist. "So what now?"

"Now we're going to talk to Riding. He's staying at the Hampton Springs Hotel."

He put the car in gear and it bounced off the curb. "Oh, wait!" she said.

He halted the car with a jerk and she opened the door to let Max and Dooley inside.

"God, not those cats again!" Chase said.

"They look tired," she said. "They need a ride."

Actually they didn't look tired. They looked excited.

"Odelia! You were right!" Max cried. "Riding was in town the night Niklaus was killed. He even told one of the guards at the sweatshop that he needed to get rid of a pesky problem, and then he drove off. That was around ten o'clock."

"Did he do it, Odelia?" asked Dooley. "Did he kill Skad?"

She couldn't very well answer that with Chase in the car. One day she might tell him about the cats, but not now. Not when he was convinced she was working with some secret informant.

"She can't talk with us in front of Chase, Dooley," Max said.

"Why not? Chase is a nice guy. He'll understand."

"No, he won't. He might be nice, but he's also just a guy."

"He's not just a guy. He's Odelia's guy," Dooley insisted stubbornly.

She smiled. "While you were finally realizing I'm always right, I had a word with my informant," she said.

"Oh? And what did they say?"

"Riding was definitely involved with the sweatshop."

"Yeah, he came out here all the time," Max chimed in.

Chase grinned. "Your cats are talking again, Odelia. It's so funny."

"Don't mind them," she said. "The night Skad was killed, he was in town. And I'm sure the sweatshop workers and the guards will be able to confirm that."

"I'll talk to the NYPD officer in charge. He'll be happy to hear it."

Chase had switched on the police siren and the blinkers and they were roaring through town, moving at a healthy clip. It only took them ten minutes to arrive at the hotel and Chase swung his car into a parking spot reserved for VIPs, right next to a black Tesla.

"There's something I haven't told you yet," Chase said as he cut the engine. "You know the best part?"

"No, what?"

He smiled. "Remember Abe found a fortune cookie in Skad's stomach? Well, the sweatshop was full of the stuff. Bags and bags of them." He popped a fortune cookie out of his pocket and handed it to her. "See how it says ZR?"

"Ziv Riding," she said slowly, turning the cookie over in her hands. "But how did it get into the victim's stomach?"

Chase shrugged. "Only thing I can think of is that Riding gave Niklaus the cookie and he ate it. And then Riding killed him."

"But wouldn't the cookie have been chewed to pieces? I thought Abe said the cookie was still intact?"

Chase frowned. "So?"

"So I think Riding shoved that cookie down Skad's throat and choked him with it."

Chase stared at her. "You have a devious mind, Odelia Poole. And you may just have solved our murder!"

"Odelia is brilliant," Dooley said.

"Yeah, she is," Max agreed.

They got out and walked to the hotel. Now the only thing they needed to do was make Ziv Riding confess. How difficult could that be?

They walked up to the lobby and Chase showed the clerk his badge and asked which room Ziv Riding was staying in. The hotel tapped a few keys. "Room five twenty-five. The Royal Suite. Mr. Riding always uses that suite when he's in town."

Odelia and Chase shared a look. "Can you check a date

for me?" Chase asked, and gave him the date Niklaus Skad was murdered.

"No, he didn't stay with us that night," said the clerk.

"Thanks," said Odelia. That would have been too easy.

"Do you know if Mr. Riding is in right now?" Chase asked.

"You'll find Mr. Riding by the pool," said the clerk.

They thanked him and walked through the lobby, through the restaurant and out to the pool, which was the heart of the hotel.

"We keep ending up here," said Chase as they stepped onto the flagged patch that lined the pool.

"That's him," said Odelia, pointing. "Right there."

Riding had just hoisted himself up out of the pool, water streaming from his sculpted body in rivulets, and was stroking the water from his hair. He walked over to a chaise lounge and stood basking in the sun. He looked like a man who hadn't a care in the world. Or a man with great lawyers.

"Well?" asked Chase. "Let's have a word with Mr. Riding, shall we?"

The fashion designer looked up when a shadow fell across his face. "You're blocking my sun," he said kindly. "Please remove yourselves." Then he recognized Odelia. "Oh, it's you again. I already told you to make an appointment with the PR department. I'll gladly talk to the media but not without an appointment. I think I made that abundantly clear."

Chase flashed him his badge. "Odelia may be a reporter, but she's also a civilian consultant helping me work a case."

The man stared at the badge. "And who are you?"

"My name is Kingsley. Chase Kingsley. Detective for the Hampton Cove Police Department."

The designer rolled his eyes. "Oh, dear. Look, I told you people I had nothing to do with this abominable sweatshop business. And you can rest assured that heads will roll once I find out who did. I don't condone this kind of thing."

"We're not here to talk about your sweatshop, Mr. Riding," said Odelia.

"We're here to talk about Niklaus Skad," said Chase.

"Oh, for goodness' sakes. I didn't even know the man. I watched his crass show from time to time, but that's as far as our association went."

"So he didn't send you an email threatening to reveal your 'dirty little secret?'" Chase asked.

The designer pursed his lips. "You know what? I don't think I'm going to talk to you at this moment, Detective. I seem to remember that everything I say can and will be used against me, so I'll leave the pleasure of talking to you people to my lawyer, who's more used to this sort of thing."

"You have a right to an attorney," Chase agreed.

"You sure do," Odelia said. "And the first thing your attorney will tell you is that it wasn't smart to drive that nice black Tesla of yours all the way up to Tucker's Farm."

"Or to park it right behind *Fry Me for an Oyster*," Chase added.

"Oh, yes. Your car was seen that night, Mr. Riding."

"We even have a witness who overheard you telling one of your bodyguards you needed to get rid of a pesky problem in town."

"And then there's that fortune cookie, of course," said Odelia.

"Did you know our coroner found that fortune cookie pretty much intact inside the victim's stomach, Mr. Riding?" Chase asked.

"That's impossible," Riding snapped. "A stomach doesn't stop working when a person dies. It keeps digesting."

"No, it doesn't," said Odelia with a laugh. The guy might

be a great designer, but he didn't know much about death. Simply about causing it.

The man gulped. "You found one of my fortune cookies in Niklaus Skad's stomach?"

"Yes, we did."

"Now I wonder how that got there?" Odelia asked.

"Unless you shoved it down his throat until he choked, of course," said Chase.

The man just sat there for a moment, looking out across the pool, his face devoid of expression. The sun hung low in the sky. The day was drawing to a close and the rays slanting across the pool surface shimmered and glittered brightly. Suddenly, Ziv Riding reared up from his chaise lounge and dashed away along the pool, his bare feet slapping on the paved floor. He was a quick bugger.

"Dammit," Chase grumbled, before setting out in pursuit.

Odelia watched as the cop raced after their suspect. And just when the designer had cleared the pool area, suddenly something blocked his path.

"Hey!" he cried when his feet got entangled in two small, furry objects.

Max and Dooley, for it was them, risked life and limb, but the intervention served its purpose, for the designer was forced to change course. Chase made a grab at him, but missed and almost toppled into the pool. And then, out of nowhere, a large black Portuguese Water Dog leaped at Riding and they both smashed into the pool.

The dog came back up first, and easily paddled to the edge of the pool. Stacie Roebuck, who'd been reading a book by the pool, looked horrified.

"Puck! Come back here! Bad boy!"

But Odelia joined her and said, "No, he's a good boy. A very brave, very good boy." She winked at Stacie. "He just nailed his owner's killer."

Stacie stared at Ziv Riding, who came up, spluttering and splashing. When he saw that Chase was waiting for him, he kept paddling for a while.

"You can't keep doing that forever, Mr. Riding!" Chase called out.

"Yes, I can!" the designer insisted. "And I want my lawyer! Get him out here! Right now! I'm not coming out without my lawyer!"

Chase sighed. "Suit yourself." He then dove into the pool. There was some more splashing, but finally Chase managed to collar his suspect and tow him in. He dragged him out of the pool bellowing, "Ziv Riding, you're under arrest for the murder of Niklaus Skad. Anything you say can and will be used against you in a court of law."

Odelia picked up Max and Dooley. "My heroes," she said softly.

"All we did was get in the way of a known killer," said Max.

"Yeah, no big deal," said Dooley.

"Puck is the real hero," Max added.

"And so he is," said Odelia.

They watched as a soaking wet Chase led an equally wet Ziv Riding to the hotel.

"So Mr. Riding killed Mr. Skad?" Stacie asked, just to be sure.

"Yes, he did. Your boss was threatening to expose Riding's sweatshop operation, which would have ruined his reputation with his investors and his clients."

"That little twerp killed my husband?" an irate voice interrupted Odelia. She saw that Cybil Truscott had gotten up from her chaise lounge. She hadn't even noticed she was there.

"Yes, he did," she acknowledged.

"Gah, and we just made dinner reservations," said Cybil. "I guess I better cancel our date."

"Unless you want to have dinner in prison, I suggest you do," Odelia said.

She shook her head disgustedly. "Men. Either they die on you, or they go around killing other men. I think I'm going to become a lesbian. Less trouble." She gave Stacie a lascivious glance. "Hey, gorgeous. Have we met?"

"I was your husband's assistant," said Stacie. "We've met several times. Not that you ever noticed me. And for your information, I'm not a lesbian."

"Too bad. You're pretty. Oh, well. I guess I'll just stick to men. There must be someone out there who's not a killer or about to die on me." And she stalked off, the death of her husband clearly not affecting her very powerfully.

"I never liked that woman," said Stacie.

"Me neither," Odelia confessed.

"I guess she'll inherit all of Niklaus's fortune."

Odelia smiled. "Didn't anybody tell you? Shortly before he died, Niklaus changed his will. Apparently he hated Cybil so much he didn't want to take any chances. So he left everything to Puck."

Stacie goggled at her. "Puck? But he didn't even like him."

"I'm sure he didn't. And I'm sure he was going to change his will again as soon as the divorce came through. But since he was killed before that happened..." She shrugged. "Puck is a very rich dog now." She eyed Stacie seriously. "You did take the necessary steps to transfer ownership of Puck to you, right?"

"Yes, I did. Everything was arranged through the notary yesterday."

"Good. Because I think Cybil might contest the will—and your claim."

Niklaus Skad's lawyer had revealed as much to Chief Alec

when her uncle had interviewed him. Cybil still had no idea, and Odelia thought it was better it stayed that way until the will was officially read.

She watched as Stacie settled down at the edge of the pool and hugged a very wet Puck. At least something good had come out of this, she thought.

Then Puck shook himself, spraying water all over the place. Stacie laughed, and so did Odelia and most of the other guests. Except…

"Hey! Watch that stupid mutt!" Cybil screamed. "He'll ruin my tan!"

Yep. Sometimes people got exactly what they deserved.

*W*e were all enjoying a leisurely time in Marge and Tex's backyard. There was good food on the menu, apparently, at least if I went by the cries of delight from Odelia and the grunts of appreciation from Uncle Alec and Chase. Us cats had gotten actual meat for a change, and Dooley had even gotten the chicken wings he'd been craving for. The murder case had been solved, Ziv Riding would spend a nice long stretch in prison, Odelia had postponed our yearly visit to the vet, and everybody was happy.

Well, almost everybody. Diego probably wasn't happy. There was no way of knowing for sure, of course, as he hadn't shown his face around these parts since his unfortunate run-in with Clarice. And Gran wasn't too happy, either, as her beau Leo was still strutting his stuff with Jackie Canolli. But I wasn't going to let her spoil the fun.

"So what about that Leo, huh?" Dooley asked, tucking into another bit of chicken. "Left my human broken-hearted. Maybe we should do something about him?"

"Like what? Put a horse's head in his bed? Break his legs?

Rough him up? We're cats, Dooley. We don't mess with humans."

"Unless they mess with our humans," said Dooley. "Like this guy Leo."

We were out on the porch, tucking into our bowls. I darted a quick look at Harriet and Brutus, who were out near the tree next to the hedge, smooching.

"When are they ever going to get enough of each other?" I asked.

Dooley followed my gaze and shrugged. "It's love, Max. It's beautiful."

I slowly turned to him. "It's love, it's beautiful? What happened to 'Brutus is a monster for stealing Harriet away from me?' I thought you loved Harriet."

"I do love Harriet, but I've come to realize that if you truly love a cat, you need to be happy when they're happy. You have to set them free to follow their hearts. And if Harriet's heart leads her to Brutus, well, then that's fine by me."

I stared at him. "Who are you and what have you done to my friend?"

Dooley grinned. "I'm growing up, Max, what about that? Maybe one of these days I might even have a shot with Norma."

"Oh, so that's the deal. You like Norma now."

"Well, she is pretty."

"She sure is. She's also high-maintenance."

He frowned. "What's high-maintenance, Max?"

"When a cat wants you to fetch her Swiss chocolates or else."

"I'll fetch her Swiss chocolates. I'll fetch her all the Swiss chocolates she needs," he said.

He had that dumb look in his eyes that goes along with being in love. Yeah, Dooley had it bad, I saw. So that's why he was cool with Harriet and Brutus. He'd transferred his affections to another queen. Well, maybe it was for the best. At least he wouldn't bother me with his endless moaning about Harriet.

"Don't you think she has the most beautiful eyes, Max? Like rays of sunshine? Or, better yet, golden orbs that reflect the world's early dawn?"

Oh, crap. This was even worse.

Harriet and Brutus walked up. Apparently you can't live on love alone, for Brutus barked, "Where's my meat? I thought we were getting meat? You two morons didn't eat my meat, did you? Cause if you did, there'll be hell to pay!"

"Here's your meat," I said, indicating Brutus's bowl.

"Good," he muttered. "I need meat. I'm a meat-eating cat."

"I think we've established that," I said.

He glanced up, a piece of raw liver between his teeth. "Giving me lip, Maxie? Better don't give me any lip. I'm the one that got us this meat. Without me, there would be kibble on the menu. So better pay me some respect."

I blinked. "Um, are you feeling all right, Brutus?"

"Course I'm feeling all right." He grinned at Harriet, his bloodied teeth an awful sight. "I'm feeling on top of the world, ain't that right, snuggle puss?"

"That's right, my cuddle man."

Then he dug in again.

I directed a worried look at Dooley, but he was still dreaming about Norma, his face displaying a moronic look. Well, even more moronic than usual.

I sidled up to Harriet. "Is Brutus all right? He seems... aggressive."

"He's just fine," said Harriet, darting loved-up looks at her cat. "I told him that the reason I was so attracted to Diego was because he acted like a real cat. A butch cat, if you know what I mean. Not like you and Dooley, who are just a tad too sweet for my taste." She sighed. "I love a cat who's tough and strong. A catly cat. And I think Brutus got the message loud and clear."

I groaned. "You turned him back into a bully?"

"Not a bully," she said with a look of reproach. "A catly cat."

"What does that even mean?!"

Brutus looked up. "Hey! Don't talk to my lady like that, Max. Show some respect."

"Brutus, my friend," I began.

He gave me the evil eye. "Don't go getting all soft on me again, Max. We're all catly cats together. There's no reason to get mushy." He directed a grin at Harriet. "Isn't that right, sugar lips?"

"That's absolutely right, my stud muffin," she cooed.

Brutus took me aside, and whispered, "Just play along, Max! She likes me all butch and macho so butch and macho is what she gets. Capisce?"

"But I liked you better when you were, you know, normal!"

Brutus rolled his eyes. "Haven't you ever been in love, Max?"

"Um, no?"

He punched my chest. "Fall in love, and then we'll talk again. And now don't cramp my style, buddy. I'm warning you. Don't ruin this for me."

"What are you two whispering about, Brutus?" Harriet asked.

"Just telling this chump what's what, my queen." Quieter, he hissed, "I like you, Max. I like you a lot, and I wanna thank you for what you did for me. But this is how it's gonna be from now on, got me?" Then, louder again, "You little weasel! If you talk to me like that again, I'm kicking your big, hairy, orange butt!"

And then he stalked off, leaving me staring after him, floored.

Oh, great. Instead of a real bully, now I got the Actors Studio version.

Dooley wandered over. "Don't you think Norma's fur is the color of—"

"No, I don't!" I interrupted him brutally. "And please don't talk to me about that cat again. Ever!"

Dooley stared at me, rudely awakened from his roseate dream. And as I sat there, moping, suddenly Harriet stole over to me. She gave me a gentle shove. "Maxie," she said in a sultry voice. "I never saw this side of you before. When did you become all dominant and butch?"

I stared at her. "Huh?"

She giggled, a low and seductive sound. "I like this new Max a lot better than the old one. How about we share a piece of chicken?"

This was just too much. After all this nonsense with Diego, and now Brutus, she wanted to steal my chicken? No way! "You've got your own damn piece of chicken," I snapped. "I'm not sharing mine."

"Ooh, Maxie," she cooed. "My butchy Maxie!"

And then she threw herself into my paws and kissed me!

EXCERPT FROM PURRFECT CRIME
(THE MYSTERIES OF MAX 5)

Prologue

Donna Bruce was a woman profoundly in love with herself. From personal experience she knew there was no other person as amazing as she was. She was smart, successful, beautiful, and, above all, she was kind to humans, children and dogs, which cannot be said about everyone. She was a giver, not a taker. In fact she gave so much she often wondered if people appreciated her enough.

Her kids, for instance, could probably love her more for all the sacrifices she had made. For one thing, they'd pretty much ruined her figure. After the twins were born, something strange but not very wonderful had happened to her hips. They'd never looked the same again. And when she saw what breastfeeding did to her boobs, she'd vowed never to fall into that horrible trap again.

She now carefully tucked her golden tresses beneath the pink shower cap, wrapped the white towel embroidered with her company's crest—a nicely rendered tiara—around her perfectly toned and tanned body, and stepped into the sauna cabin. She had the cabin installed only six months ago as a special treat to herself when donna.vip, the lifestyle website she'd launched a decade ago, had topped 200 million in revenue.

She languidly stretched out on the authentic Finnish wood bench, took a sip from her flute of Moët & Chandon Dom Perignon, and closed her eyes. She'd just done a conference call with her CEO and now it was time to relax. Later today she had a session with her private fitness coach scheduled, and to top it all off she was going to treat herself to a healing massage as well. Time to get pampered!

And she'd just reached that slightly drowsy state she enjoyed so much when a soft clanking sound attracted her attention. She opened her eyes and saw through the slight haze that filled the cabin that there was someone moving about outside.

She frowned, wondering who it could be. Her housekeeper Jackie wasn't coming in until ten, and the rest of the staff knew better than to intrude on her alone time. It was hard to make out the person's face, as the one small window was all steamed up. With a grunt of annoyance she got up and wiped her hand across the glass to look out. And that's when she noticed something very disturbing: the person was wearing a mask of some kind. One of those silly Halloween masks.

"What do you think you're doing?" she called out.

But the intruder just stood there, unmoving, staring at her through the black mask that covered his or her entire face.

"Who are you?" she asked. "Answer me at once!"

When the person didn't respond, she shook her head and took a firm grip on the wood door handle, giving it a good yank. The door didn't budge. She tried again, knowing that these sauna doors could be sticky, but to no avail. And that's when she saw that someone—presumably the masked person outside—had stuck a long object through the door's handle, blocking it. It was her long handle loofah, the one she'd intended to take into the sauna with her.

"Hey! This isn't funny!" she cried, tapping the pane furiously. "Open this door right now!"

And that's when the masked figure reacted for the first time by raising a hand and pointing a finger at her, cocking their thumb and making a shooting gesture. And in that exact moment, she became aware of an odd sound that seemed to come from somewhere above her head. A buzzing sound. She looked up in alarm, and when she saw the first dozen bees streaming into the sauna cabin, she uttered a cry of shock and fear.

She rapped the window again, more frantic this time. "Let me out! Why are you doing this to me?! Just let me out of here!"

More bees fluttered into the cramped space and soon started filling it. There must have been hundreds, or maybe even thousands! And as they descended upon her, she felt the first stings. She started swatting them away with her towel, but there were too many of them, and for some reason they seemed drawn to her, whipped into a frenzy by some unknown cause. And as she stumbled and fell, desperately flapping her hands in a bid to get rid of the pesky insects, she soon succumbed. Her final thought, before she lost consciousness was, "Why me?!"

Chapter One

Having spent most of the night outside, looking up at the stars and commenting to Dooley on their curious shape, attending a meeting of cat choir in the nearby Hampton Cove Park, and generally contemplating the state of the world and my place in it, I was ready to perform my daily duty and make sure my human Odelia Poole got a bright and early start on her day. I do this by jumping up onto her bed, plodding across Odelia's sleeping form, and finally kneading her arm until she wakes up and gives me a cuddle. This has been our morning ritual since just about forever.

When I finally reached the top of the stairs, slightly winded, a pleasant sound emanating from the bedroom filled me with a warm and fuzzy feeling of benevolence: Odelia was softly snoring, indicating she was in urgent need of a wake-up catcall. So I padded over, and jumped up onto the foot of the bed. At least, that was my intention, only for some reason I must have misjudged the distance, for instead of landing on all fours on the bed, I landed on my butt on the bedside rug.

I shook my head, happy that no one saw me in this awkward position. With a slight shrug of the shoulders, I decided to try again. This time the result was even worse. I never even cleared the bed frame, let alone the mattress or the comforter. Like an Olympic pole vaulter who discovers he's lost the ability, I suddenly found myself facing a new and horrifying reality: I couldn't jump anymore!

"Hey, Max," a familiar voice sounded behind me. "What are you doing?"

"What does it look like I'm doing, Dooley?" I grumbled. "I'm trying to jump into bed!"

He paused, then asked, "So why are you still on the floor?"

"Because…" I stared up at the bed, which all of a sudden had turned into an insurmountable obstacle for some reason. "Actually I don't know what's going on. The bed just seems higher now."

"A sudden weakness," Dooley decided knowingly. "It happens to me all the time."

"Well, it doesn't happen to me," I said, scratching my head.

Yes, cats scratch their heads. We just make sure we retract our claws, otherwise it would be a fine mess.

"You probably need food. Did you have breakfast? When I don't have my breakfast I feel weak. Do you feel weak?"

I gave him my best scowl. "I feel fine. And for your information, yes, I did have my breakfast. The best kibble money can buy and a nice chunk of chicken and liver paté."

"Wow, what happened?"

"What do you mean, what happened?"

"I thought Odelia only got you the cheap stuff? Why did she go out and splurge all of a sudden?"

"I guess she felt I deserved it. I have been helping her solve murder case after murder case lately."

"Me too, but I didn't get any special treats."

"You have to file your complaint with Gran, Dooley. She is your human, after all."

Dooley's Ragamuffin face sagged. "Gran has been too busy to notice me lately."

"Too busy? Why, what's she been up to?"

"Beats me. She's been receiving packages in the mail. A lot of them. In fact Marge and Tex are pretty much fed up with her. Seems like they're the ones who have to pay for all those packages."

Perhaps now would be a good time to make some introductions, especially for the people who haven't been following my adventures closely. My name is Max, as you have probably deduced, and I'm something of a private cat sleuth. Since Odelia is a reporter and always in need of fresh and juicy stories, I'm only too happy to supply them. My frequent collaborator on these outings is Dooley, my best friend and neighbor. Dooley's human is Vesta Muffin, Odelia's grandmother who lives next door. Dooley is my wingcat. My partner in crime. Between you and me, Dooley is not exactly the brightest bulb in the bulb shop, so it's a good thing he's got me. I'm smart enough for the both of us.

"Why don't I give you a paw up?" Dooley asked now.

"I don't know..." I muttered. I glanced behind Dooley, making sure he was alone. If we were going to do this, I didn't want there to be any witnesses.

Dooley followed my gaze. "What are you looking at?" Then he got it. "Oh, if you're looking for Harriet, she was fast asleep in Brutus's paws. Those two must have had a rough night."

My face clouded. Being reminded of Brutus usually has a souring effect on my mood. You see, Brutus is what us cats call an intruder. He came waltzing into our lives a couple of weeks ago and has refused to leave ever since. He belongs to Chase Kingsley, a cop Odelia has taken a liking to, but seems to spend an awful lot of time next door, cozying up to Harriet, Odelia's mom's white Persian.

I made up my mind. "Let's do this," I grunted. If we didn't, Odelia might wake up of her own accord, and I'd miss my window of opportunity to put in some much-needed snuggle time.

Dooley padded up to me and plunked down on his haunches. "How do you want to do this?"

"Simple. I jump and you give me a boost."

"You mean, like, on the count of three or something?"

"Or something." I got ready, poised at the foot of the bed and said, "One—two—"

"Wait," Dooley said. "Are we doing this on three or after three?"

"What do you mean?"

"Do I boost you on three, or right after?"

"Why would you boost me right after? The count of three usually means the count of three, Dooley."

"So, one, two, three and boost? Or one, two, three, pause, and then boost?"

"One, two, three, boost," I said, starting to lose my patience. "Now, are we doing this or not?"

He thought about this for a moment, a puzzled look on his face. "Do you want to do this?"

"Of course I want to do this! Preferably before we die of old age."

Dooley's eyes went wide. "Die of old age? Do you think we're dying, Max?!"

"No, we're not dying! I just want to put in some snuggle time, is that so hard to understand?"

"Oh, right," he said, understanding dawning. "I thought you said we were dying."

For some reason Dooley has been obsessing about dying lately. Usually I can talk him out of it, but then he sees something on TV and the whole thing starts all over again.

"Are you ready?"

Dooley nodded. "I'm ready, Max."

"One—two—"

"Wait!"

I groaned. "What is it now?"

"Where do I boost you?"

"Up the bed! Where else?"

"No, I mean, do I boost your butt or your hind paws or what? I'm new to this boosting business," he explained apologetically.

"It's not exactly an Olympic discipline, Dooley. There are no rules. You can boost me wherever you want." On second thought… "Though stay away from my butt."

"Right. Stay away from your butt. So where…"

"Anywhere but my butt! Now one—two—"

"Max!"

"What?!"

"What if I boost you too hard and you end up flying across the bed and down the other side?"

I fixed him with a hard look. "Trust me, Dooley, the chances of that happening are slim to none. I mean, look at us. I'm like the Dwayne Johnson of cats and you're more like Andrew Garfield in *Hacksaw Ridge*, all scrawny and mangy. You'll be lucky if you can boost me a couple inches, which is all I need," I hastened to add.

"Do you think I'm too mangy?" asked Dooley with a frown.

"Not too mangy. You're just thin is all. A very healthy thin."

"Not a sickly thin? Like an I'm-about-to-die thin?"

Oh, God. I did not need this aggravation. "Absolutely not. More like a my-name-is-Gwyneth-Paltrow-and-I'm-willowy-and-gorgeous kind of thin."

"I thought you said I looked like Andrew Garfield?"

"In a very Gwyneth Paltrow-y way."

This seemed to please him, as he gave me a grateful smile. "Why, thanks, Max. That's the nicest thing you've ever said to me."

"Great. Now about that boost?"

"Oh! Right! I forgot all about that."

"Focus, Dooley. Now, are you ready?"

"Ready," he said, his face a study in concentration.

"One—two—three—"

"Boost!" he cried and placed both paws on my butt, giving me a mighty shove.

And... we had liftoff! Only it didn't last very long, nor did it carry me where I was aiming to go. Instead, I plunked right back down again, landing on top of Dooley, who ended up squeezed beneath my sizable buns.

There was a momentary pause, while we both figured out

what went wrong, then Dooley croaked, "Can you please lift your butt, Max? You're choking me!"

Applause broke out behind us, and a loud cackling sound, and when I looked up, I saw we'd been joined by Harriet and Brutus. The latter was applauding, a Draco Malfoy-type sneer on his mug, and Harriet was doing the cackling, apparently finding the whole scene hilarious.

"What's so funny?" I asked with an angry look at the newly arrived.

"You!" Brutus cried. "You're so fat you can't even jump on the bed!"

"I'm not fat! I'm just... experiencing some issues with my takeoff."

"Issues with your takeoff! You're not an airplane, Max. You're a cat. A cat too fat to fly!" Harriet dissolved into giggles while Brutus was laughing so hard his belly shook.

"Max!" Dooley breathed. "You're... choking... me..."

I released Dooley by lifting my butt, then resumed my scowling. "I'm not fat—I'm big-boned. There's a difference. And Odelia probably bought a new bed, that's all. I never had any trouble jumping into the old bed, which was still here yesterday morning. Isn't that right Dooley?"

But Dooley was still catching his breath, taking big gulps of it.

"That's the exact same bed as always," said Brutus. He narrowed his eyes at me. "Girlfriend stealer."

I rolled my eyes. "Here we go again."

Brutus had walked up to me and poked my chest with his paw. "You kissed my girlfriend, Max. I saw you so don't try to deny it."

"I didn't kiss anyone! She kissed me!"

"That's what you say."

"Because that's what happened!"

He leaned in and dropped his voice to a whisper. "I thought we had an understanding, Max. I thought you and I were friends. And then you went and did a thing like that." He pursed his lips. "You're despicable. There's no other word for it."

"I didn't kiss her," I hissed. "She kissed me. I'm not even interested in Harriet!"

"What are you two whispering about?" Harriet asked with a laugh.

"Nothing, honey bunch," said Brutus in his sweetest voice. "Just clearing up some stuff."

"Max is right, Brutus," Dooley loud-whispered. "Harriet kissed him, not the other way around. And he didn't even like it, did you, Max?" These last words were spoken with a look of reproach in my direction. Dooley has always fancied Harriet, and he cannot grasp being kissed by that divine feline and not enjoying the experience.

"I heard you," said Harriet, tripping up deftly. "And for your information, I didn't kiss Max."

"See?!" Brutus exclaimed triumphantly.

"My Inner Goddess did."

"What?!"

Harriet raised her chin defiantly. "I can't be held responsible for every little thing my Inner Goddess does, Brutus. Sometimes she wears a blindfold. I thought I was kissing you, actually. I only realized my mistake when I reached out and the only thing my paw met was a yielding fluffiness where rock-hard muscles should have been."

Brutus stared at her. "Go on."

She placed a paw on his chest and closed her eyes. "See, now that I'm feeling your steely pecs I know it's you. That was my mistake. I kissed first and touched later."

I groaned loudly. "Yielding fluffiness?!"

"Shut up, Max," said Brutus. "Watch and learn."

And then the two of them locked lips. Instinctively I held

up a paw to cover Dooley's eyes. He did not have to see this. He seemed to appreciate the gesture, for he didn't slap my paw away. He only asked, when the smooching sounds finally abated, "Is it over yet?"

"Yes, it is," I said, lowering my paw. Harriet had kissed me, no doubt about it, but if it made her feel better to lie to both herself and to Brutus, it was fine by me. I didn't need Brutus going back to his old bullying ways. This détente we had going for us suited me fine, so I was happy when finally the kissing stopped and Brutus slapped me on the back.

"And that's how you do it, buddy!"

"Great," I muttered. "Now, can you give me a boost? I need to wake up Odelia."

"Sure thing," said Brutus, suddenly in an expansive mood. And as I got ready to take the leap again, he got into position directly behind me, not unlike a running back. And before I could initiate the launch sequence, Brutus was shouting, "Hut one—hut two—hut three—go!"

I made the mighty jump and... "Owowowow!" Brutus, instead of giving me a regular boost, had dug his nails into my behind! The result was that I flew up onto the bed and landed right on top of Odelia's sleeping form, and it wasn't a soft landing either.

"Ooph!" Odelia grunted, when a flying blorange obstacle landed squarely on her stomach. She stared down at me. "Max! Where's the fire?!"

I gave her a sheepish look. "Wakey-wakey."

I directed a scathing look at Brutus, who gave me a grin. "See, Max? I knew you could do it!"

Chapter Two

"So then Brutus gave me a boost and that's how I ended

up on your stomach," I finished my account of the recent events.

Odelia, who's blond and petite with the most strikingly green eyes, tied the sash of her bathrobe and gave me a worried look. "I better make that appointment with Vena. I knew I should never have put it off."

My eyes widened to the size of saucers, which for us cats is considerable, since our eyes are a lot smaller than a human's eyes to begin with. "Not Vena!"

"Yes, Vena. With everything that's been going on I totally forgot to make a new appointment but it's obvious now that she was right all along." She placed a comforting hand on my head. "You're overweight, Max. Totally overweight, and I've got no one else to blame but myself."

"I'm not overweight. I'm just… big-boned. It runs in the family."

"It's for your own good," she said. "If you don't start dieting again, you'll just get in trouble."

"I won't get in trouble, I promise!" I cried. Anything not to have to go to Vena, who is just about the vet from hell. For some reason she loves sticking me with needles and suggesting to Odelia that she feed me kibble that tastes like cardboard. The woman is my own personal tormentor.

"It's not your fault," Odelia said as she started down the stairs. "I indulge you. I keep buying those snacks that you like so much and I probably overfeed you, too."

"No, you don't," I said, desperate now. I trotted after her, my paws sounding heavy on the stairs. "I only eat the bare minimum as it is. In fact I'm always hungry."

She paused and listened to the pounding my paws made on the stairs. "You hear that? That's not normal, Max. You're not supposed to walk like that."

"Like what?" I asked, pausing mid-step.

"Like an elephant trampling in the brush."

"I don't sound like an elephant trampling in the brush," I said indignantly, but made an effort to tread a little lighter. Only problem was, it's hard to tread lightly when you're going downhill. Gravity, you know.

"And Vena said that when you get too big it's bad for your heart. Fat tissue builds up around the organ and that's not a good thing."

"My heart is just fine," I promised, tapping my chest. "Healthy as an ox!"

"And you look like one, too," said Brutus. The black cat was right behind me, and obviously enjoying the conversation tremendously.

"I've booked you an appointment, too, by the way, Brutus," said Odelia now.

We'd reached the bottom of the stairs and she walked into the kitchen to start up the coffeemaker. How people can drink that black sludge is beyond me, but then a lot of stuff humans do makes no sense at all. Like putting a perfectly healthy cat on a diet!

"Me!" cried Brutus. "Why me?!"

"Because Chase told me he doesn't remember the last time you went. So it might as well have been never." She frowned. "Though you are neutered, so you must have gone at least once."

A deep blush crept up Brutus's features. At least I think it did. It was hard to be sure with all that dark hair covering his visage. He cut a quick look at Harriet, who pretended she hadn't heard. "I, um—I'm sure that's not possible," he said now.

"That you're neutered or that you didn't go to the vet in years?" Odelia asked deftly, taking a cup and saucer from the cupboard over the sink.

Brutus appeared to be shrinking before my very eyes, a sight I enjoyed a lot, I have to say. "Both," he said curtly, now actively avoiding Harriet's cool gaze.

"Don't worry, Brutus," said Dooley. "We're all neutered. Max is neutered. I am neutered. Even Harriet is neutered. Isn't that right, Harriet?"

"None of your beeswax," Harriet snapped.

"Beeswaxed?" asked Dooley. "I'm pretty sure the right word is neutered."

"Dooley!" Harriet said with a warning glare.

"What? What did I say?"

"Oh, come off it, you guys," said Odelia, crouching down. "It's nothing to be ashamed about. If you weren't neutered I'm sure we'd have a fresh litter every couple of months, and we can't have that now, can we?"

"I don't see why not," Harriet muttered. It was obviously still a sore point.

"Because I can't take care of so many cats," Odelia said softly. "You see that, don't you?"

"Yeah, just do the math," said Dooley. "Three litters a year times eight kittens a litter that's..." He frowned, looking goofy for a moment, then said, "... a heck of a lot of cats!"

"It is," said Odelia. "And I'd just end up having to bring them to the shelter. And I don't need to tell you what happens to cats that end up at the animal shelter, do I?"

"They are adopted by loving humans?" Dooley ventured.

"They die, Dooley," Brutus growled. "They all die."

Dooley uttered a cry of horror and staggered back a few paces. "No, they don't!"

"Oh, yes, they do. And then they're turned into sausages and people eat them!"

"Brutus!" Odelia said. "Don't scare Dooley." She gave Dooley a comforting pat on the back. "They're not turned into sausages. But they're not adopted, either, I'm afraid. At least not all of them. Though I'm sure a lot of them find warm and loving families."

"See!" Dooley cried triumphantly. "They're all placed with their very own Odelias!"

"Thanks," said Odelia, rising to her feet. "Now about Vena…"

Lucky for us the bell rang at that exact moment, and Gran came rushing in through the glass sliding door, looking like she was about to lay an egg.

"Is he here?!" Gran croaked anxiously. "Is he here?!"

"Is who here?" asked Odelia, moving to the front door.

"The UPS guy, of course!"

Gran is a white-haired little old lady, but even though she looks like sweetness incarnate, she's quite a pistol.

"See?" asked Dooley, turning to me. "This is what I told you."

"What did you tell me?" I asked. The morning had already been so traumatizing my mind had actively started to repress the memories.

"About Gran ordering a bunch of stuff online and Marge and Tex having to pay for it."

Odelia had opened the door and Dooley was right: a pimply teenager in a brown uniform with 'UPS' on his chest stood before her, a big, bulky package in his hands. "Vesta Muffin?" he asked.

"That's me!" Gran squealed and darted forward, grabbed the package from the teenager's hands and ran to the living room with it.

Odelia signed for the package and sent the kid on his way. "What's going on, Gran?" she asked.

"Oh, nothing," said Gran, eagerly tearing open the package.

We all gathered around, and since it's hard to see anything from the floor, we all hopped up onto the chairs to have a good look at this mysterious package.

Gran, licking her lips, finally succeeded in ripping away the packaging, and before us lay three shiny green eggs. Huh.

"Gran," said Odelia in her warning voice. It's the voice she likes to use when me or Dooley have been up to no good, which, obviously, practically never happens.

"What?" asked Gran innocently. "I need them. I'm dating again."

What a bunch of green eggs had to do with dating was beyond me, but, like I said, humans are weird. And in my personal experience no human is weirder than Gran.

"You're dating again?" asked Odelia. "I thought that after Leo you were done with all of that."

Leo was a horny old man that Gran used to run around with. We kept bumping into them in the weirdest places, practicing the weirdest positions. All very disturbing.

"Done with dating?" asked Gran indignantly. "Oh, the horror! How can anyone be done with dating? Didn't anyone ever tell you that sex only gets better with age?"

"Like a fine wine," said Dooley, though I doubted he knew what he was talking about.

"The only thing that doesn't improve is my hoo-hee. Which is why I need these."

"What is a hoo-hee?" asked Dooley innocently.

Odelia blushed slightly. "Nothing you should concern yourself with, Dooley."

"You don't know what a hoo-hee is?" asked Gran, raising an eyebrow. "What about hoo-ha? Lady bits? Fine China? Lady garden? Vajayjay?"

Dooley shook his head. "Doesn't ring a bell."

Gran laughed. "You're funny, Dooley. Doesn't ring a bell. I'll bet it doesn't ring your bell, but it sure as heck rung Leo's bell, and there's plenty of Leos out there."

"I'll just bet there are," Odelia muttered, picking up one of the green eggs. "So how do you use these?" Then she noticed four pairs of cat eyes following her every movement and she put the egg down again. "Never mind. I'm sure I don't want to know."

"And I'm sure you do," said Gran. "If you want to entertain your fellow you need to practice the fine art of the jade egg, honey."

"Something to do with energy and healing, right?" asked Odelia with a frown.

Gran threw her head back and laughed. "Of course not! It's all about training those pelvic muscles. You want to get a good grip on your fella's…" She cast a quick look at Dooley. "… fella. Increase the pleasure—his and yours. Trust me," she said as she placed one of the green eggs in the palm of Odelia's hand, "you'll make your man very, very happy."

"That happy, huh?" asked Odelia as she rolled the smooth green egg in her hand.

"Happier," said Gran as she let the other two eggs disappear into the pockets of her dress. She gestured at the box. "Can you let this disappear, honey? Your mom and dad don't need to know."

"Wait a minute," said Odelia. "You're not going to have this… stuff arrive here from now on, are you?"

"Of course I am. I hate to break it to you, Odelia, but your parents are ageists. They think just because I'm old I'm all shriveled up down there." She patted her granddaughter on the cheek. "Nothing could be further from the truth. In fact I'm pretty sure I get more nookie than those dried-up old prunes."

"Hey, that's my parents you're talking about."

"I know, which is why I'm so glad you're nothing like them. You wouldn't stand in the way of your grandmother enjoying her golden years, would you?"

"No, but…"

"Of course you wouldn't." She gave Odelia a fat wink.

"Stick around, kid. You may learn a trick or two from this old dame."

And with these words, she practically galloped through the sliding door and disappeared into the garden, no doubt eager to start practicing those eggs on her hoo-hee, whatever a hoo-hee was.

For a long moment, silence reigned, then Odelia said, "Right. I think I'll just put that egg away, shall I?"

"So what is it for, exactly?" asked Harriet.

Odelia produced an awkward smile. "Decorative purposes?"

Harriet narrowed her eyes at her. "A decorative egg is going to make Chase very, very happy?"

"Yes, it will," Odelia trudged on bravely. "Chase likes a nicely decorated... room."

She was backtracking towards the staircase, and we all watched her go. Then, suddenly, she turned around and popped up the stairs. We heard her rummage around in her bedroom, a drawer opening and closing. Those drawers contained a lot of funny-looking stuff. Amongst other things, they also contained a small battery-powered rocket, though I had no idea why Odelia would need a pocket rocket in her bedroom.

Moments later, she returned, still that sheepish look on her face.

Humans. They're just too weird.

Just then, the doorbell rang again.

"More eggs?" asked Harriet acerbically.

But when Odelia went to open the door, it was her uncle. Chief of Police Alec Lip. Like me, Chief Alec is big-boned. And, also like me, he's a great guy. Always ready with a smile or a kind remark, which makes him real popular with the locals. He wasn't smiling now, though, and when he opened his mouth to speak, it soon became clear why. "There's been a murder. A really nasty one."

Chapter Three

Odelia put the four cats in her old Ford pickup and followed Uncle Alec as he set the course in his police cruiser.

"So who died?" asked Max, who'd crawled up on the passenger seat, as was his habit when there was no one else in the car. No other humans, at least.

"A woman named Donna Bruce," said Odelia, anxiously peering through the windshield. "She's the one who sold Gran those green eggs."

"She's a farmer?" asked Max.

"No, she's not a farmer. She's a former actress who now runs a lifestyle website. A very popular one." She shook her head. "I don't know what's happening in this town. It's just one murder after another. If this keeps up, no tourists are going to want to come here anymore."

"Why did Uncle Alec say it was a nasty murder?" asked Dooley from the backseat.

"Because the woman was murdered in a gruesome way."

She could hear Dooley gulp. Gran's cat was a sensitive plant when it came to things like murder, and she was starting to wonder if it was such a good idea to bring him along. Max, she knew, could handle himself, and so could Brutus and Harriet. But Dooley was the baby of the cat menagerie, and sometimes got spooked by his own shadow. "Maybe you better wait in the car, Dooley," she suggested. "While the others snoop around."

"But I want to snoop around, too," said Dooley. "I love snooping around."

She smiled. That was obvious. All her cats loved snooping around, which was why she took them along in the first place. They often talked to other pets, or even pets that belonged to the victims, and had proved invaluable when ferreting out clues.

Her uncle Alec was aware of this unique talent. Chase? Not so much, though by now he was used to this quirky side of her personality. He even thought it was cute. She'd never told him she could communicate with her cats, though, and probably never would. He might not take it too well.

She thought about Chase and a warm and fuzzy feeling spread through her chest. She'd never thought she would fall for the rugged cop but she had. And by the looks of things, he liked her, too, which was a real boon. They even shared a comfortable working relationship now, which was very different from the way things were when they first met. The burly cop, a recent transplant from the NYPD, wasn't used to nosy reporters investigating a bunch of crimes alongside him. Fortunately she'd quickly proven her worth, and now he was more than happy to allow her to tag along.

As if he'd read her mind, Max asked, "So how are things between you and Chase?"

"Yeah," Harriet chimed in. "When are you going to get married?"

She saw how Max and Dooley shared a quick look of panic and laughed. "Hold your horses, young lady. Who said anything about me and Chase getting married?"

"It's all over town," said Harriet with a shrug. "All the cats are talking about it."

"Which means all the Hampton Covians are talking about it," Max said.

That was true enough. The Hampton Cove cat community was like a barometer of the human community. She blushed slightly. "So what are they saying, exactly?"

"Well, that the wedding will take place later this year, though it might be sooner rather than later because the first baby is already underway." The gorgeous Persian screwed up her face. "What is a shotgun wedding, Odelia?"

Odelia's blush deepened. "A shotgun wedding? Is that what they're saying?"

All four cats nodded. "I think it means that everybody brings a shotgun to the wedding," said Brutus knowingly.

"Don't be an idiot," said Max. "Why would anyone bring a shotgun to a wedding? That's just dumb."

"Who are you calling dumb, fatso? They're obviously bringing shotguns to make sure nobody crashes the wedding. Duh."

"Crashes the wedding?" asked Dooley. "Is that even a thing?"

"Didn't you see that movie last week? *Wedding crashers*? Two guys go around crashing weddings and having a blast," said Brutus.

"Until they fall in love and get married themselves," said Harriet. "I thought it was the most romantic thing ever. Though I didn't like that they portrayed Bradley Cooper as such a nasty person. I like Bradley Cooper. He's so handsome and cute."

"He's not that handsome," said Brutus. "His mouth is too big for his face."

"It is not. His mouth is just the right size."

"The right size for what?" scoffed Brutus. "To load a Big Mac in one bite?"

"Listen, you guys," said Odelia, interrupting this fascinating discussion of Bradley Cooper's face. "For one thing, Chase and I are not getting married. And for another, I'm not pregnant so there won't be a shotgun wedding."

"That's too bad," said Harriet, her face falling. "I was looking forward to being a bridesmaid."

"That's impossible," said Max. "Cats can't be bridesmaids. That's just preposterous."

Harriet narrowed her eyes. "What are you saying, Max? That I wouldn't make a wonderful bridesmaid? For your information, I would be the perfect bridesmaid. I don't even have to wear a dress. I'm beautiful just the way I am."

Odelia smiled. "That's true. And if I ever get married, you guys will all get to come."

Max groaned. "Do I have to? I hate weddings. Everybody is always crying. Those things are even worse than funerals."

"People are crying because they're happy, Max," said Odelia. "Those are happy tears."

"I don't get it," said the blorange cat. "Why cry when you're happy? That doesn't make sense."

"Yes, it does," said Harriet. "You wouldn't understand, though, Max. And that's because you're a Neanderthal."

"No, I'm not," said Max. "I'm a cat, not a Neanderthal."

"What's a Neanderthal?" asked Dooley.

"It's a kind of old human," said Max. "With a lot of hair and a big mouth."

"Like Bradley Cooper," said Brutus.

"Bradley Cooper is not a Neanderthal!" Harriet snapped. "Bradley Cooper is gorgeous."

"More gorgeous than me?" asked Brutus, stung.

Harriet's face softened. "Of course not, cutie pie. Nobody can be more gorgeous than you."

"Maybe *you* should have one of those shotgun weddings," Max grumbled. "So I can bring a shotgun and shoot myself."

"We're here," said Odelia cheerfully, cutting off all this nonsense about a shotgun wedding. She just hoped those rumors hadn't reached her mother's ears. Nobody likes to hear about their daughter's supposed pregnancy and forced wedding because of gossip. Then again, maybe it was a good thing. If people thought she and Chase were about to get married, she should probably take it as a compliment.

Though the town's gossip mill was obviously getting a little ahead of itself this time around.

True, there had been a lot of kissing lately, but things hadn't progressed beyond that. Yet. Did she want them to go beyond that stage? Maybe. Did Chase want to? She had absolutely no idea. Chase was one of those strong, silent types. The ones that don't wear their hearts on their sleeves. Beyond those kisses they had yet to address whatever it was that was going on between them. Heck, he hadn't even asked her out. Maybe he never would? Maybe those kisses were just a way of showing his appreciation for all she'd done for the community? Maybe it was an NYPD thing: instead of shaking hands, NYPD cops simply kissed their colleagues. It was definitely not something she'd ever seen on *NYPD Blue*. Then again, they never showed everything on those shows.

She parked right behind her uncle's squad car and got out, allowing the four cats to jump from their respective seats.

"Let's go, guys," she said. "You know the drill. Talk to witnesses. Try to find out what happened here."

She watched the cats traipse up to the house and smiled. Her own personal feline detective squad. She wouldn't know what to do without them.

She watched her uncle take off his sunglasses and take in their surroundings. Donna Bruce had done well for herself, that much was obvious. The house was built in hacienda style, with a low red-tile roof and stuccoed orange outer walls.

"Nice place," said Uncle Alec admiringly. "Though more like something one would expect in the Hollywood Hills than out here in Hampton Cove."

"Isn't Donna originally from Los Angeles?"

"She is. She only moved out here to put some distance

between herself and her ex-husband. And because her company is headquartered in New York."

"This is such a coincidence," Odelia said as she watched the police activity around the house. Half a dozen squad cars were haphazardly parked on the circular driveway, and an ambulance stood, lights flashing, indicating the coroner was already there.

"What is?" asked her uncle, hoisting his pants over his bulk and patting down his few strands of hair.

"Just this morning a package arrived from donna.vip for your mother."

Chief Alec closed his eyes. "God, not again. I thought Marge put a stop to that nonsense."

"What nonsense?"

"Didn't she tell you? Your grandmother has been ordering those packages for weeks now. She's addicted to that Donna crap. And the worst part? Your mom has been footing the bill as Vesta doesn't have a credit card. Marge told me she's up to five grand now."

Odelia's jaw dropped. "Five grand!"

"Yeah, for a bunch of useless stuff. According to Marge she even bought one of those steamers for her, um, well, you know what."

Odelia frowned. "A vegetable steamer?"

Uncle Alec suddenly looked uncomfortable. "Not exactly. She uses it on her… business."

"Her business?"

He heaved an exasperated groan. "Her lady parts, all right?"

Odelia smiled. "She bought a vaginal steamer?" Uncle Alec grumbled something under his breath as he stalked off. She hurried to keep up with him. "No wonder Mom is mad. That stuff must cost a fortune."

"And it's not as if she needs it," said her uncle. "I mean,

she's seventy-five, for crying out loud. What does she need a vaginal steamer for?"

"Well, she does have a very active sex life."

Uncle Alec winced. He directed a pleading look at his niece. "Please, Odelia. I don't need to hear all that."

Which was probably why Mom had allowed this buying frenzy to go on as long as it had. Nobody wanted to sit down with Gran and have a serious conversation about her sex life. It wasn't a topic one simply launched into.

"I'll talk to Gran," she promised. "Tell her to ease up on the spending."

"You do that," her uncle grumbled.

They walked into the house and Odelia admired her surroundings. Donna Bruce had taste, that much was obvious. The foyer had a homey feel, with its hardwood floors, soft pink wallpaper and white lacquered furniture. And as they progressed into the living room and then the kitchen, she had to admit she wouldn't mind living in a place like this. Selling jade eggs and vaginal steamers had obviously been very lucrative for the founder of donna.vip.

They reached the spa area, where a small indoor pool awaited them, along with the sauna cabin where Donna's housekeeper had found the body of her employer that morning.

"You better prepare yourself for a shock," said Uncle Alec. "It's not a pretty sight."

She braced herself and stepped into the sauna. Donna Bruce was lying on the floor, partly covered by a towel, her face swollen beyond recognition. Every part of her body that was visible had suffered the same fate. The woman had literally been stung to death.

She swallowed. "How—how did they get the bees in here?"

Uncle Alec gestured at the fan that was placed in the ceiling. "They reversed the airflow and placed an entire batch of bees on top of it. The little beasties must have been pretty pissed off when they were propelled past the fan's blades and into this extremely hot environment. They simply attacked the first thing they came into contact with. Which was Donna Bruce."

"I'm guessing she died from anaphylactic shock," said the coroner, who was standing in a corner, picking up the body of a dead bee and dumping it into a plastic baggie. Abe Cornwall was a shabbily-dressed man with frizzy gray hair but he was an ace medical examiner. "Though judging from the state of the body, she might have died from the venom itself. She must have sustained thousands of stings in a matter of minutes."

"This entire cabin was full of bees when the housekeeper arrived," Uncle Alec explained. "Thousands and thousands of them."

"And there's no question whether this was an accident or not?" asked Odelia.

"No way," another male voice spoke.

She turned around with a smile, and got a small shock of pleasure when she found herself gazing into the green-flecked blue eyes of Chase Kingsley. He filled the entire doorframe with his muscular physique, and the cabin with his powerful presence. "So it was definitely murder, huh?"

"Definitely," said Chase with a smile of greeting.

"I'll let you two kids come up with a theory as to who's responsible," said Uncle Alec. "I have to talk to the ex-husband about what to do with the kids."

"The kids?" asked Odelia.

"Yeah." Uncle Alec frowned at his notebook. "Sweetums and Honeychild. Good thing they weren't here when it happened."

"Oh, those poor babies," said Odelia.

"Big babies," said Uncle Alec. "Sweetums and Honeychild are six." He shook his head. "Who gives their kid a name like that?"

"Donna Bruce," said Chase, staring down at the victim. He glanced up at the chief. "So am I in charge of this thing, Chief?"

"Yes, you are," said Chief Alec. "Along with Odelia—in an entirely unofficial capacity, of course."

Chase gave her a grin. "Looks like the gang is back together, babe."

She returned his smile. "Yay."

ALSO BY NIC SAINT

Nora Steel

Murder Retreat

The Kellys

Murder Motel

Death in Suburbia

Emily Stone

Murder at the Art Class

Washington & Jefferson

First Shot

Alice Whitehouse

Spooky Times

Spooky Trills

Spooky End

Spooky Spells

Ghosts of London

Between a Ghost and a Spooky Place

Public Ghost Number One

Ghost Save the Queen

Box Set 1 (Books 1-3)

A Tale of Two Harrys

Ghost of Girlband Past

Ghostlier Things

Charleneland

Deadly Ride

Final Ride

Neighborhood Witch Committee

Witchy Start

Witchy Worries

Witchy Wishes

Saffron Diffley

Crime and Retribution

Vice and Verdict

Felonies and Penalties (Saffron Diffley Short 1)

The B-Team

Once Upon a Spy

Tate-à-Tate

Enemy of the Tates

Ghosts vs. Spies

The Ghost Who Came in from the Cold

Witchy Fingers

Witchy Trouble

Witchy Hexations

Witchy Possessions

Witchy Riches

Box Set 1 (Books 1-4)

The Mysteries of Bell & Whitehouse

One Spoonful of Trouble

Two Scoops of Murder

Three Shots of Disaster

Box Set 1 (Books 1-3)

A Twist of Wraith

A Touch of Ghost

A Clash of Spooks

Box Set 2 (Books 4-6)

The Stuffing of Nightmares

A Breath of Dead Air

An Act of Hodd

Box Set 3 (Books 7-9)

A Game of Dons

Standalone Novels

When in Bruges

The Whiskered Spy

ThrillFix

Homejacking

The Eighth Billionaire

The Wrong Woman

ABOUT NIC

Nic Saint is the pen name for writing couple Nick and Nicole Saint. They've penned 70+ novels in the romance, cat sleuth, middle grade, suspense, comedy and cozy mystery genres. Nicole has a background in accounting and Nick in political science and before being struck by the writing bug the Saints worked odd jobs around the world (including massage therapist in Mexico, gardener in Italy, restaurant manager in India, and Berlitz teacher in Belgium).

When they're not writing they enjoy Christmas-themed Hallmark movies (whether it's Christmas or not), all manner of pastry, comic books, a daily dose of yoga (to limber up those limbs), and spoiling their big red tomcat Tommy.

Sign up for the no-spam newsletter and be the first to know when a new book comes out: nicsaint.com/newsletter.

www.nicsaint.com

16933662R00142